William A Pratt

The Yachtman and Coaster's Book of Reference

William A Pratt

The Yachtman and Coaster's Book of Reference

ISBN/EAN: 9783337410315

Printed in Europe, USA, Canada, Australia, Japan

Cover: Foto ©Andreas Hilbeck / pixelio.de

More available books at **www.hansebooks.com**

THE YACHTMAN AND COASTER'S

BOOK OF REFERENCE,

GIVING COURSES AND DISTANCES, WITH THE RELATIVE BEARINGS
OF THE LIGHT HOUSES AND LIGHT SHIPS, FROM CAPE
HATTERAS TO ST. JOHN'S, N. B., WITH RELIABLE
SAILING DIRECTIONS FOR SEVENTY-FIVE
HARBORS AND PORTS.

AS COMPILED FROM THE LATEST U. S. COAST SURVEYS.

BY

WM. A. PRATT.

HARTFORD, CONN.:
PRINTED BY THE CASE, LOCKWOOD & BRAINARD COMPANY.
1878.

INTRODUCTION.

THE author of this work, in an experience of nearly thirty years coasting and yachting, has often, in common with every other coast sailing master, felt the need of some suitable reference-book which would correctly answer the multitude of questions that are constantly arising with reference to courses, distances, bearings, etc., on the part of yachtmen and amateur sailors. The work is the result of the most careful and thorough research and study of the latest and best United States coast surveys, confirmed in nearly every important feature from his own personal experience and observation. He has aimed at correctness and simplicity, rather than finish and polish, hence has no apology to offer for any want of literary merit which the critical may readily discover.

I expect this book to be appreciated by my fellow-craftsmen the yachtmen and coasters, for the convenient form in which this information is packed, giving, as it does, the distances in all cases, with the courses and bearings from one point to another. It will be found a very desirable companion at night, when it is almost impossible to get a light to bear on a chart.

All men of experience know how hastily and imperfectly these things are taken off at night, even when it is possible to do it at all; and there are times when wet with fog or rain, that to handle a chart with any degree of correctness is almost impossible; thus having these matters principally in my mind when compiling these Descriptions, Directions, Courses, and Bearings, I have tried to talk with those whom I would direct, in a manner so plain as not to be misunderstood. The book is worth all that it will cost as an educator of the *eye* in judging distances. This is a faculty that every captain should cultivate, and as I here give distances with the courses and bearings, by making it a subject of comparison with your own judgment, a person can become very accurate in their estimation of distances.

Hoping, therefore, that this book will meet the approval of those for whom it is designed, I now commit it into the hands of the toilers and pleasure-hunters of the *deep*.

WM. A. PRATT.

All Courses and Bearings given are Magnetic; the Distances are given in Nautical Miles.

A Nautical Mile is 6,082 feet.
A Statute Mile is 5,280 feet.

DESIGNATIONS ON CHARTS AND BUOY LISTS.

R., red buoys, Nos. 2, 4, 6, etc., starboard.

B., black buoys, Nos. 1, 3, 5, etc., port.

P. S., white and black perpendicular stripes, without numbers, in mid-channel.

H. S., red and black horizontal stripes (on obstructions), without numbers.

INDEX.

The Index to this Book is embraced in the alphabetical arrange-
ment of the Lighthouses and Light Ships that are mentioned in
writing out these Directions and Bearings. As it is often necessary
to refer to one light several times when writing out these Directions, this Index will serve a four-fold purpose, viz.: Character of
Light shown, its Order of Lens, Height above the Sea, and the
Fog Signal in use.

REFERENCES.

F. W., - - - -	- Fixed white.
F. R., - - -	- Fixed red.
Flg. W., - - -	- Flashing white.
Flg. R., - - -	- Flashing red.
Flg. R. & W., - -	- Flashing red and white.
F. V. W. F., - -	- Fixed white, varied by white flashes.
F. V. R. F., - -	- Fixed white, varied by red flashes.
F. V. R. & W. F., -	- Fixed white, varied by red and white flashes.
F. R. V. R. F., -	- ·Fixed red, varied by red flashes.
[1 ⊙], - - -	- First-order lens apparatus.
[2 ⊙], - - -	- Second-order lens apparatus.
[3 ⊙], - - -	- Third-order lens apparatus.
[4 ⊙], - - -	- Fourth-order lens apparatus.
[5 ⊙], - - -	- Fifth-order lens apparatus.
[6 ⊙], - - -	- Sixth-order lens apparatus.

NOTE.

If any doubt arises as to which Light is meant, as there are several of the same name, it will only be necessary to look at the page given in the Index, and it will give the position of the Light so that there need be no mistake as to the character or position of any Light referred to in the book. It would hardly be possible to arrange these Lights in a more convenient form for a ready reference than the plan here given.

Whoever will study the Book carefully, will find very little to mystify, and an amount of information that every man sailing the coast desires to know. W. A. P.

COURSES, DISTANCES, AND BEARINGS,

BEGINNING AT GOVERNOR'S ISLAND, NEW YORK.

Eastward.—From the NE. side of Governor's Island to the Light on the East end of Blackwell's Island, the distance by the river is 6¼ miles, and its direct bearing is NE. It would be of no benefit to give the courses in detail through the East River. From Blackwell's Island Light to the North Brother Light, the distance is 2½ miles; from this to Throgg's Point Light, the course is E. ¼ S., distance 5 miles; Stepping Stone Light bears from Throgg's Point NE. ½ N., distance 1⅞ miles.

Execution Light bears from the Stepping Stone NE. ¾ N., distance 3⅝ miles.

Directions for Entering the Head of the Sound.—When running for Execution Light, keep it within the bearings of W. ½ N., to SW. ½ W., passing it on your starboard hand; keeping nearer to this than the Sand's Point Light; when in past the Execution Light, steer SW. ¼ S., or you can keep the Stepping Stone Light (red) open a little south of Throgg's Point Light, as that will take you clear of Gangway Rock and Hart Island Point. Leave the Stepping Stone on your port hand, then steer S. SW. until to Throgg's Point, which you will give a good berth in rounding; when you can steer W. by N. about one mile, then W. ½ S. will take you to Riker's Island.

You can pass the Execution Light to the North of it, but give the reef a good berth on that side. This reef bears NE. by N. ¼ N., and SW. by S. ¼ S., therefore do not approach the Light on those bearings. The South end of Hart Island bears from Execution Light SW. ¼ S., distance 2½ miles. Gangway Rock buoy bears from Execution Light S. SW., distance 1¼ miles.

If bound into Hempstead Bay from the Westward, or bound West from there, do not get the Execution Light to bear anything North of W. by N., on account of the Old Hen Rock, which bears from the Light about E. SE., distance 1⅛ miles, and from Sands' Point Light, E. by N. ¼ N., distance ⅞ of a mile.

This rock shows little before low water. Sometimes there is a bush on it, but it should be supplied with an iron spindle.

LONG ISLAND SOUND, LONG COURSES.

From Sands' Point Light to Race Rock Light, the distance is 80⅔ miles, as follows : An E. NE. course, distance 8⅞ miles, when Captain's Island Light will bear NW. The course from this bearing to Race Rock Light is E. ¼ N., distance 71½ miles. This is the longest course you can make in the Sound. From one-half a mile North of Sands' Point to Stratford Point Light, bearing North, distance one mile, the course is E. NE., distance 32½ miles ; from this to Little Gull Island Light the course is East, distance 45 miles.

LONG ISLAND SOUND LIGHTS, WITH THEIR RELATIVE BEARINGS AND DISTANCES, INCLUDING SOME SPECIAL DIRECTIONS FOR HARBORS.

Captain's Island Light bears from Sands' Point Light NE. ¼ N., distance 8⅜ miles.

Huntington, or Eaton's Neck Light, is distant from Execution and Sands' Point Lights 16¼ miles. The buoy off Lloyd's Point bears from Eaton's Neck Light W. ¾ N., distance 4 miles. Eaton's Neck bears from Captain's Island Light E. by S. ½ S., distance 10½ miles.

Lloyd's Harbor Light bears from Eaton's Neck SW., distance 2⅞ miles. Norwalk Island Light bears from Execution Light NE. by E. ½ E., distance 17¾ miles ; and from

Eaton's Neck it bears N. ½ W., distance 5¾ miles. Stratford Shoal Light bears from Eaton's Neck E. by N. ⅛ N., distance 14⅞ miles, and from Norwalk Island Light it bears E. ½ S., distance 14⅜ miles.

Directions to Norwalk Harbor Anchorage.—Bring the Light to bear NE. by E. ½ E., and run for it until you are about 1¼ to 1½ miles from it, then steer North until past the red buoy on Green's Ledge, which bears from the Light E. NE., distance 1¼ miles ; after passing this buoy about one-quarter of a mile, steer E. NE. until the Light bears South, or a little West of it, when you will have from 10 to 13 feet of water at low tide.

Old Field Light bears from Norwalk Island Light E. SE., distance 14¼ miles. Old Field bears from Eaton's Neck Light East, distance 12⅝ miles. Stratford Shoal Light bears from Old Field N. by E. ¼ E., distance 4¾ miles.

Mt. Misery Shoal buoy bears from Old Field Light E. by N., distance 1¾ miles (6 feet on this shoal).

Penfield Reef Light bears from Eaton's Neck NE., distance 13 miles, and from Norwalk Island Light E. by N. ½ N., distance 10 miles. Be careful and not get Penfield Reef, or Norwalk Island Lights, in the line of this bearing, only when you are between two and four miles West of Penfield Reef ; when you can run into Southport, which is a tide harbor. To go in there, run to the northward until you make the beacon, pass that on your starboard hand, then keep the breakwater end on your starboard bow, and haul around it on that hand. It is a good place of refuge, if in a small craft. Stratford Shoal Light bears from Penfield Reef SE. ¼ E., distance 6½ miles.

Stratford Point Light bears, from Penfield Reef Light, E. by N. ¼ N., distance 5½ miles.

To Enter Black Rock Harbor.—From the Westward, after passing Penfield Reef Light about one-fourth of a mile, steer N. by W. ¼ W. about 1⅛ miles, or until the Light bears East, then

2

steer about North, and anchor with the Light bearing from
E. SE. to SE.   You will pass a red buoy when going in, that
lies about three-eighths of a mile South from the Light.   If
you are from the Eastward, run in for the Light, and give
the point a good berth, as above directed.

Black Rock Light bears from Penfield Reef N. by E., distance 1½ miles.

Directions for Entering Bridgeport Harbor.—When Bridgeport Light bears N. ½ E., run for it, passing it on your port
hand; continue on this course until up past a red buoy,
and to a beacon which you leave on your port hand; from
this steer NE. ½ N. to another beacon, which you leave on
the same hand; after passing this beacon a short distance,
the course is about NW. by N., but the buoys must be your
chief guide.

Bridgeport Light bears from Penfield Reef NE. ½ N., distance 2⅞ miles, and from Black Rock Light E. NE., distance
1⅞ miles.   The mean rise and fall of the tide at Bridgeport
is six feet five inches.

Southwest Ledge, or New Haven Light, bears from Old
Field Light NE. ½ N., distance 17⅞ miles.   New Haven Light
bears from Stratford Shoal NE., little Easterly, distance 13¾
miles.

Stratford Point Light bears from Stratford Shoal Light
N. ½ E., distance 5¾ miles.

New Haven Light bears from Stratford Point E. NE.,
distance 10 miles.

Falkner's Island Light bears from Stratford Shoal E. by
N. ¾ N., distance 22⅞ miles, and from Stratford *Point* Light it
bears E. ¼ N., distance 20½ miles.

Horton's Point Light bears from Stratford Shoal E. ½ S.,
distance 29¾ miles.   Horton's Point bears from New Haven
Light SE. by E. ¼ E., distance 22¾ miles   Horton's Point

bears from Falkner's Island SE. ¼ S., distance 11⅞ miles. Falkner's Island Light bears from New Haven E. by S. ½ S., distance 11¼ miles; Branford Beacon is about on this bearing, distance from New Haven Light 5 miles, and from Falkner's Island Light 6¾ miles.

Directions for Entering New Haven Harbor.—The Southwest Ledge, or New Haven Light, may be approached close to on all sides except in the direction E. by N., where there are rocks, varying from 150 to 350 yards distant, having from 10 to 13 feet of water over them at low tide. When coming from the Westward, bring this Light to bear NE. by E., and run for it until you are within one-fourth or one-eighth of a mile of it; then steer N. by E. ½ E., distance 2¼ miles, when you will be up to Fort Hale Point, and near the Red Buoy No. 6, which you leave on your starboard hand; then steer N. ¾ W. about three-fourths of a mile to Black Buoy No. 5, from this N ¾ E. towards the end of Long Wharf, on which there is a red light. The best place to anchor is SW. from the end of this wharf.

When running for New Haven Light from the Eastward, do not get the Light to bear West of W. NW., as this bearing will take you clear of all the shoals up to the Light, and outside of Branford Reef. You can haul in to the East of the Light, but pretty near to it, if your draft of water is not over ten feet.

The mean rise and fall of the tide at New Haven is six feet.

THIMBLE ISLANDS.

This is truly the most charming and romantic combination of land and water that is to be found on the shores of Long Island Sound.

I will give some general directions to enter the harbor. If you are from the Westward, and pretty well in to the land East of New Haven Light, steer East, and you will make a red buoy that is on Negro Heads; leave it on your port hand, and continue E. ½ N. (you should have the Outer Thimble on your starboard bow), you will soon make another red buoy,

which is distant from Negro Heads 1½ miles; this buoy is on
Inner Reef, and it bears from Outer Thimble W. by N. ¼ N.,
distance ¼ mile, pass it on your port hand, and after passing
this buoy, haul up to NE. ½ E., and run in, keeping nearer to
the islands on the starboard hand; after you have passed three
islands on the starboard, beside the little *Outer Thimble*,
anchor about N. NE. from the end of the last of the three. If
you haul in just East of Branford Beacon, steer NE. by E.
until you make the red buoy on Inner Reef. On this course,
you will pass the black buoy on Wheaton's Reef on your starboard hand; this buoy bears from Inner Reef buoy S. ¼ W.,
distance ¼ of a mile. If coming from the Westward, and
well in North of Falkner's Island, steer W. by N. for the
Outer Thimble, give it only a little berth, and haul in the
West side of the islands, and proceed as before directed.

From Falkner's Island East, to pass North of Cornfield
Point, Middle Ground. *Cornfield Point Light Ship* is anchored
off the South side of this shoal. From one-half a mile North
of the black buoy on the North point of Falkner's Island, an
E. ¼ S. course will take you just south of the red buoy on the
tail of Saybrook Bar. From close in to the South side of
Falkner's Island an E. ¼ N. course will take you to the same
place, passing North of the middle ground on these courses.
This sand shoal extends about 5½ miles East and West, with
depth of water on it from 7 to 18 feet. *The Light Ship* is about
off the middle of the shoal.

To avoid the shoal when South of it, do not bring *Cornfield
Point Light Ship to bear South of East when West of it, or South
of West when East of it.* When to the Northward of this shoal
at night, care must be taken that Saybrook Light does not
bear East of E. by N. ¼ N.; when you are East far enough to
bring *Cornfield Light Ship* to bear SE. or South of it, Crane's
Reef bears W. by S. from Saybrook Light, distance 2⅜ miles,
and from *The Light Ship* NW. ½ N., distance 2⅓ miles.

The Hen and Chickens Reef, on which there is a spindle,
bears from Crane's Reef E. ¼ N., distance ¾ of a mile. Corn-

field Point buoy bears from this spindle E. ½ S., distance ¾ of a mile.

There is a good passage North of these three reefs by keeping from one-eighth to one-fourth of a mile North of them; but there is a reef that is bare at ¾ ebb, which bears from the end of Cornfield Point W. ½ N., distance ⅝ mile, and from Hen and Chickens spindle NE. by N. ½ N., distance nearly ½ a mile. *Westbrook Harbor* is to the Northward of Crane's Reef; Salt Island bears from this reef N.NW., distance 1¾ miles.

There is a dangerous rock called the Dumpling, that bears about SW. by W. from Salt Island, distance ⅜ of a mile; therefore to avoid it, run in toward the island until about West of it, when you can haul to the Westward and anchor opposite the East Cottages.

Cornfield Point Light Ship bears from Falkner's Island E. ¼ S., distance 12 miles, and from Horton's Point it bears N.NE. ¼ E., distance 8¾ miles. Saybrook Light bears from *Cornfield Light Ship* NE., distance 3¼ miles. Saybrook Light bears from Horton's Point Light NE. by N. ¼ N., distance 12⅛ miles.

Plumb Island Light bears from Saybrook SE. ¾ S., distance 8⅜ miles. *Bartlett's Reef Light Ship* bears from *Cornfield Light Ship* E. ½ N., distance 12 miles, and Little Gull Island Light bears E. by S. ¼ S., distance 12¾ miles. Little Gull bears from Saybrook Light SE. by E. ½ E., distance 11⅛ miles.

Directions for Entering Connecticut River by the East Channel.—First, make the P. S. or entrance buoy that bears SE. ¼ E. from Saybrook Light, distance 1¾ miles, then run in, keeping the Light on or near this bearing, *i. e.*, NW. ¼ W., passing the Stone Beacon on your port hand about 200 or 300 feet distant; from this steer N. by W. ½ W. up past the steamboat docks to the anchorage North of the docks. Keep well on the West side of the river up this far. If bound to the river from the Westward, inside of Cornfield Shoal, bring Saybrook

Light to bear E.NE., and run for it on that bearing until well in to the breakwater, and when Saybrook Light bears North, steer for it, passing close by the East side of the West breakwater; run in between the two breakwaters, and as you approach the Light, enter the river about midway of the Light and the Beacon. Then observe the other directions. This entrance to the Connecticut River is very plain. Seven feet of water can be carried in here at any time of tide, except in extreme cases. Strangers should not attempt to enter this river at night.

Little Gull Island Light bears from *Bartlett's Reef Light Ship* S. ¾ E., distance 4⅛ miles. Race Rock Light bears from Little Gull Light NE. by E. ¼ E., distance 3½ miles. Valiant Rock, with 17 feet of water on it, lies about in the middle of the Race; it bears from Little Gull E.NE., distance 2 miles, and from Race Rock Light it bears SW. ½ W., distance nearly 1⅓ miles. The flood tide runs about NW. by W. in this part of the Race, at about 4 knots on the 2d quarter. The rips in the Race are very heavy, with the wind against the tide. *Bartlett's Reef Light Ship* bears from New London Light SW. ½ W., distance 3⅛ miles.

To Enter New London Harbor from the Westward.—After passing *Bartlett's Reef Light Ship*, steer NE. by E. ¾ E., until New London Light bears N. ½ E.; you will then keep the Light within the bearings of N. ½ E. and N.NW. until within ¼ or ⅜ of a mile of it; then keep N. by E., or the East shore best aboard. The anchoring ground is above the fort, on the West side of the river.—Little Gull Island Light bears from New London Light S. by W. ¼ W., distance 6½ miles. Race Rock Light bears from New London Light S. by E. ½ E., distance 4¾ miles. This is to be a Flashing Red Light when lighted.

To enter New London Harbor from Fisher's Island Sound.—When the Sea Flower Beacon bears SW., distance ¼ of a mile, New London Light will bear NW. by W. ¼ W.; keep the Light on this bearing, and run for it until about three-eighths of a mile of it, when you will steer about North. On this course you will first pass a red buoy off Pine Island, on your starboard hand, and then the buoy and beacon that is on Black Ledge on your port. This course will take you North of the horizontal striped buoy on Frank's Ledge, but you can leave it on either hand, only give it a little berth.

The Sea Flower Beacon mentioned above bears NW. ¼ N., distance ¾ of a mile from the Dumpling Light.

GARDINER'S BAY, L. I.

From Gardiner's Point Light to Greenport, the distance is 10 miles. To Sag Harbor from Gardiner's Point, distance 10¾ miles. Plumb Island Light bears from Gardiner's Point NW. ¼ W., distance 3½ miles. Long Beach Point Light bears from Gardiner's Point W. ½ S., distance 7¼ miles. Long Beach Point bears from Plumb Island Light SW. ¾ W., distance 5¾ miles.

Sailing Directions for Greenport.—If coming through Plumb Gut, after passing the Beacon on Orient Reef, steer SW. ¼ S. until Long Beach Point Light bears NW. by W., when you will pass little North of a P.S. or channel buoy; from this a W.NW. course until West of the Light, is perfectly safe for most any vessel; but a W. by N. course will take you to the next P.S. or channel buoy, and from that a NW. ¼ N. course will take you to the Light bearing East; you can then steer about W. ½ S., and pass close by Hay Beach Point, (port hand,) then W.SW., passing a red buoy on your starboard hand. The best anchorage for yachts is from South to S.E. of the railroad wharf.

PLUMB GUT.

If you wish to go through Plumb Gut in the night, from the Eastward (inside, or past Gardiner's Point), do not haul up for the Gut until Plumb Island Light bears N.NW., then merely give the Island a berth of 100 or 200 yards distance. A good breeze is necessary here for safety, on account of the strong tide and the rips it makes.

FOR SAG HARBOR FROM PLUMB GUT.

Steer S. by W. until Cedar Island Light bears SW. by W. ½ W., then steer that course, leaving the Light as you approach it on your port hand; then steer S. ¾ W. about 1¼ miles; then you will haul more to the Westward, and be guided by the color of the buoys, red starboard, and black on your port hand.

If you wish to enter Gardiner's Bay past the East end of Plumb Island, you should either keep pretty close to the Island, or go to the East of Old Silas Rock, which is always above water. About one-fourth of a mile NW. from this rock there is the wreck of a government steamer, and parts of her are pretty near the surface at low tide. The ship channel is to the Eastward of Old Silas; 8½ fathoms of water will be carried through there.

Bedford Reef bears S. ¾ E. from Old Silas Rock. It has thirteen feet of water on it. Marked by a buoy.

Directions to find Napeague Harbor in the night.—After passing the extreme East point of Gardiner's Island (a point that is very rocky, and it should be allowed a good berth), steer about South, keeping Little Gull Light just on the edge of the bluff on Gardiner's Island, which will bring you to the mouth of the harbor. *To Enter Napeague Harbor.*—When you pass the outer or entrance buoy, leave it on your port hand, and steer about S. by W. until you pass another buoy or bush on your port, then haul to the Southward, and keep well toward the East shore as you enter. Keep a lookout for the shoals on the West side of the entrance.

Do not keep off to the Westward after you are in the Bay, until you are nearly to the middle Fish Factory.

FISHER'S ISLAND SOUND.

North Dumpling Light bears from New London Light SE. ¾ E., distance 3⅝ miles. Mystic Light bears from North Dumpling NE., distance 2¼ miles. *Eel Grass Shoal Light Ship* bears from North Dumpling E. by N. ¼ N., distance 3⅝ miles. Stonington Light House bears from the *Eel Grass Light Ship* E.NE., distance 2½ miles. Watch Hill Light bears from the Dumpling West, distance 7¼ miles.

Directions for Stonington Harbor.—From one-fourth of a mile South of *Bartlett's Reef Light Ship*, an E. ¾ N. course will carry you a little North of North Dumpling Light ; continue on this course until to the *Eel Grass Shoal Light Ship*, and when little past her, steer for Stonington Light, keeping it on your port bow ; the course will be about NE. ¼ E., distance 2⅛ miles. You will pass a *red buoy* on your *port hand* on *this run.* When about one-fourth of a mile of Stonington Light, keep N. by E. ½ E. toward the West end of the Breakwater, North of which you can anchor, or continue on and anchor above the steamboat wharf.

STONINGTON FROM THE EASTWARD.

Steer W. ¾ N. in past Watch Hill Light, passing South of it not less than ¼ of a mile ; passing the Gangway Rock buoy (red), on your starboard hand.

The Watch Hill Reef Buoy and Spindle will be on your port ; continue on the above course, passing Naptree Point Buoy (red) on your starboard hand, and when Stonington Light bears North steer for it open on your starboard bow, passing it from ⅛ to ¼ of a mile distance. South by West, distance ¼ of a mile from the Light, you will pass an H.S. Buoy on your starboard hand. (See other directions.)

FISHER'S ISLAND SOUND.

From little South of *Bartlett's Reef Light Ship* steer E. ½ N. until well past the Dumpling Light, then steer East until near to Naptree Point Buoy (red) then steer E. ½ S. out past the Gangway Rock Buoy, passing it on your port, and the Watch Hill Spindle and Buoy on your starboard hand. The tide runs so strong through this Sound, that a given course cannot be relied on, but a careful attention must be paid to the Buoys and Spindles.

I will give the Buoys and Spindles as passed on this course from Dumpling Light to Watch Hill.

You will first pass a Red Buoy on Ram Island Reef; North of the Buoy is a Spindle on the same Reef; these you will leave some distance on your port hand. The next on your port will be the Spindle on Latimer's Reef, the West end, and an H.S. Buoy on the East end of the same Reef. This Spindle bears SE. by E., distance ⅔ of a mile from *Eel Grass Shoal Light Ship.* Southwest ½ South from Latimer's Reef Spindle is a Black Buoy on Young's Rock, and S. by E. from the same Spindle is a Black Buoy on Seal Rocks. East by South from the Seal Rock Buoy is the Spindle on Wiccopesset Reef, and E. ¼ S. from this is a Spindle on Catumb Reef.

These two Black Buoys and the two Spindles, to be passed on your starboard hand ; but before you are to the last Spindle named, you will have to pass Naptree Point Buoy (red), on your port hand. This Buoy bears from Catumb Reef Spindle NW., distance ⅔ of a mile. You will next pass on your port the Gangway Rock Buoy, and on your starboard hand, Watch Hill Reef Spindle and Buoy.

Watch Hill Light bears from New London Light E. by S., distance 10¼ miles.

From *Watch Hill Light to Point Judith* the course is East, distance 17½ miles.

Montauk Point Light bears from *Little Gull Light* SE., distance 14 miles. To pass Montauk Point from Little Gull Island Light, steer SE. ½ E. until Montauk Point bears South, then merely give the Point a good berth in rounding it.

On this course given, you will pass West of Cerebus Shoal buoy, and East of Shagwong Reef. This Reef bears from Montauk Light NW. ½ N., distance 3¾ miles. The SW. end of Block Island bears from Little Gull Light E. by S. ½ S., distance 22½ miles, and Block Island North Point Light bears E. ½ S., distance 24¾ miles. Point Judith Light bears from Little Gull E. ¾ N., distance 30 miles; Watch Hill Light bears from Little Gull E.NE. ¼ E., distance 12⅝ miles.

This bearing is directly across the Watch Hill Reefs that lie to the Southward of the Light. Point Judith bears from Watch Hill Light E. ¼ N., distance 1.7½ miles. Montauk Light bears from Watch Hill S. ¾ W., distance 13⅞ miles; Block Island North Point Light bears from Watch Hill SE. by E. ¾ E., distance 13⅝ miles. Point Judith Light bears from Montauk Point NE. ¾ E., distance 29¼ miles. Block Island North Point Light bears from Montauk NE. by E. ½ E., distance 15⅞ miles, and from Gardiner's Point E. ¼ N., distance 26¼ miles. This bearing is over Cerebus Shoal, which lies 8½ miles from Gardiner's Point, 7¼ miles E.SE. from Little Gull Light, and 7½ miles NW. by N. ½ N. from Montauk Point. Block Island Light on the SE. Point bears from Montauk Point E. by N., distance, 15 miles.

This course will take you over SW. Ledge, which is distant from Montauk Point 9¼ miles, and from Block Island Light 5¾ miles. The least water on SW. Ledge is 5 fathoms, and in heavy weather it breaks.

Sometimes codfish and bluefish are plenty on this Reef. If you wish to go into Block Island Harbor, you can keep within one-eighth of a mile of the Island on the South side of it, haul to the Northward as you get East of the Light, and run for the Gap, or end of the breakwater, on your port bow, passing it on that hand. There is good anchorage Northwest of the breakwater, and the Basin can accommodate a large number of small craft.

There are two Range Lights to show the line of the breakwater. They bear N.NE. and S.SW. from each other, and when coming in here in the night, keep the high or rear light open West of the front low light. The outer end of the breakwater curves to the Northward, and when it is finished, probably these lights will mark the extreme end of it when they are in range. If you want to try the codfishing, you will generally find them about E.SE. from the breakwater, distance 5 to 7 miles; but if you are not fitted with the gear, you will always find one of the Islanders ready to go with you and furnish lines and bait at a reasonable price.

The buoy off the North Point of the Island bears from the Light N. ½ E., distance 1⅜ miles.

I will say for Block Island that I think it surpasses all other places *on the coast West of the Isle of Shoals,* as a summer resort, on account of its pure ocean air, cool nights, good fishing and sailing, and good hotels. The Ocean View will be found a pleasant and well-kept house, as its proprietor intends to please all who dwell with him. [This is no advertisement.]

Point Judith Light bears from Block Island North Point Light NE. ½ N., distance 9 miles, and from the SE. Point Light it bears NE. by N. ½ N., distance 12½ miles, and 11¾ from the breakwater on the same bearing.

Beaver-tail Light bears from Block Island Southeast Point Light NE. by N. ¼ N. distance 19 miles.

Beaver-tail bears from Point Judith NE. ¼ N., distance 6½ miles. If bound up to Newport or the East passage from near Point Judith, steer NE. ¼ E. until you are above Beaver-tail Light, then run NE. ½ E., and if bound up the Bay, when Rose Island Light bears N.NE., steer N. ½ E., passing it on your starboard hand. If you are bound up the Bay by the West passage, when around Point Judith, steer NE. ½ N. until up to Beaver-tail, when you will steer N. by E. up past Dutch Island Light, which is distant from Beaver-tail 2⅞ miles. If you wish to stop at Dutch Island Harbor, when about an eighth of a mile below it steer NE., passing near the Light on your port hand, you will pass a red buoy on your starboard. (You can enter this Harbor from the Northward.) After you are to the North end of Dutch Island, and bound up the Bay, steer N. by E. ¼ E. until Warwick Neck Light, which is distant from Dutch Island 10⅜ miles, bears N. ¼ E., then run for it until it is distant three-eighths of a mile, then steer NE. Other directions for this Bay will be seen.

Brenten's Reef Light Ship bears from the North point

Block Island Light NE. ½ E., distance 15¼ miles. *Brenten's Reef Light Ship* bears from Point Judith NE. by E. ¼ E., distance 6¾ miles, and from Beaver-tail it bears SE. by S. ¼ S., distance 1½ miles. Brenten's Reef Buoy bears from Beaver-tail Light E.SE., distance 1¾ miles.

If bound into Newport from the Eastward, bring Beaver-tail Light to bear NW. by W., and run for it on this bearing; this will take you some distance North of the *Light Ship*, and one-fourth of a mile South of the Reef buoy; the *Light Ship* lies little over one mile SW. ½ W. from the end of the Reef. When you are about one mile from Beaver-tail Light, the *Light Ship* bearing S.SW., haul up to N.NE., and run nearly two miles, or until you are above Castle Hill, which is the extreme West point of land on your starboard hand; it bears from Beaver-tail E. by N. ½ N., distance 1½ miles.

(Jan., 1878, there is an Automatic Whistling Buoy 200 yards W. by S. from Castle Hill, only to serve as a fog signal. If it does not remain, it will be substituted by a fog signal station on the shore near this point.)

You will then steer N. by E. ½ E., which course will take you past the Fort Dock; go as close to this as you like. The course from this dock to a black buoy off the South end of Goat Island, is SE. by E. ¼ E.; leave this on your port hand, passing North of Lime Rock Light, which bears from Fort Adam's Dock SE. ¾ E., distance ⅝ of a mile. If the wind is not favorable to enter the harbor this way, you can go around the North end of Goat Island, and haul in past the Light on the Breakwater, then steer S. ½ W. until past the Old Colony Steamboat Dock.

Choose your anchorage, if possible, out of the line of the steamboats' passage to their docks, and East of the N. Y. Steamers' course, which is directly from their dock to Lime Rock Light. Then, if you are in want of anything in the ship chandlery line, call on friend Coggeshall, on the American Steamboat Co's Dock.

BEARINGS AND DISTANCES WITH SOME SAILING DIREC-
TIONS FOR NARRAGANSETT BAY.

Rose Island Light bears from Beaver-tail NE. ¾ E., distance
3¾ miles, and from *Brenten's Reef Light Ship*, NE. by N.,
distance 4¼ miles. (Both of these bearings range across the
land.)

The South end of Gould Island bears from Rose Island
Light N. ¾ E., distance 2 miles. When Rose Island bears
East one-eighth of a mile, the course to Sand Point Light (on
the East side of Prudence Island) is NE. by N. ½ N., distance 7 miles. From near Sand Point Light, a NE. ½ E. course,
distance 2⅝ miles, will take you between the Muscle Shoal
and Bristol Ferry Lights. On this course you will pass near
a black buoy off the SE. point of Hog Island. This buoy
bears from the Muscle Shoal Light W. by S. ¼ S., distance
½ a mile.

From north of the Muscle Shoal Light, to the Beacon off
Fall River, the course is NE. by E., distance 5⅝ miles. If you
are bound to Bristol, after passing the Hog Island buoy, steer
N. ½ W. until up to the wharves, distance a little over two
miles. On this course you will first pass a red buoy near
Bristol Ferry Light, and a black buoy, about three-fourths of
a mile above the point buoy; the next is an horizontal striped
buoy nearly up to the town, this you leave on your port hand.

Sailing Directions for Bristol West of Hog Island.—When
the red buoy off the SW. point of Hog Island bears East,
steer N. by E. ¾ E., distance 1⅜ miles, to a black buoy. (On
this course you will pass the Castle Island Beacon on your
right.) When up to the black buoy, steer NE. for the Town,
passing West of the horizontal striped buoy.

The red buoy on the SW. point of Hog Island, bears from
Sand Point Light NE. ¼ E., distance 1¾ miles.

If bound to Warren, after passing Sand Point Light, steer
North; this course will carry you to the East of Ohio Ledge
buoy, distant from the Light 4⅜ miles, and when this buoy

bears West, steer NE. ¼ E. leaving the buoy on the South end of Rumstick Shoal on your port hand. This buoy lies from Ohio Ledge buoy, distance 1⅜ miles. You will next pass a black buoy on your port as usual; on this course you will pass three red buoys on your starboard hand, and Allen's Rock Beacon on your port, then above this beacon, about NE. ¼ E. from it, you will pass on your port, a black buoy on the SE. end of the Middle Ground; above this you will pass three red buoys on the starboard hand, course about N. by E. The distance from the beacon to the upper red buoy is about ⅞ of a mile. Keep a good look-out for the Upper Middle Ground.

There is good water up to the Town, and with a careful attention to the buoys, these directions can be relied on if you have no chart.

PROVIDENCE, FROM NEWPORT.

From the Breakwater Light on the North end of Goat Island a N. by W. course will take you clear of all the reefs, and West of Bishop's Rock buoy. The first buoy above the Light is a black one on Tracey's Ledge, East of that is a red buoy on Patrick's Rock, then the black buoy North of the Gull Rocks. On these rocks there is a small beacon; you will leave this on your port hand.

The *Bishop Rock* buoy bears from the *Gull Rocks* buoy N. ¾ E., distance ¾ of a mile.

When up to this buoy (Bishop Rock), a N. ¼ E. course, distance 5⅜ miles, will carry you up to Despair Island bearing West. This island lies off the NE. end of Hope Island, and Hope Island bears N. by E. ½ E., distance 1½ miles, from the north end of Conanicut Island. On the above course given, *i. e.*, N. ¼ E., you will pass the Halfway Rock Spindle on your starboard hand. It bears from the Bishop Rock buoy N. by E., distance 2¾ miles. (There is a passage between the South end of Prudence Island and Halfway Rocks of over one-half a mile.) You should give Hope Island a good berth on all sides. When Despair Island bears West, steer N. ½ W. for Warwick Light, distance 3½ miles, until the Light is about one-quarter or three-eighths of a mile distant, then the course is NE. ¾ N., distance nearly three miles, to a black buoy on the shoal South of Conimicut Point Light; the buoy bears from this Light S. ½ E., distance ¾ of a mile. From this buoy steer North until past the Light, then NW. by N. ½ N., distance 1⅜ miles, to the Light on Bullock Point Shoals, which you leave on your starboard hand. From this Light to the Light on the oyster beds (or Sabine's Point Light) the course is N. ¾ W., distance 1⅜ miles; you will leave this Light on your starboard hand, and the Pawtuxent Beacon on your port; continue the course past the Light about one-fourth of a mile, then steer NE. ¼ N., passing a red buoy on your starboard hand, then a black buoy on your port; continue on this course until the Light on Pomham Rock bears N.NE., then steer for it, passing it on your starboard hand, and Pomham Beacon on your port. From near this Light (West of it) the course is N. by W., until nearly up to the Light on Fuller's Rock, distance 1⅛ miles; this Light you will leave on your starboard hand.

Off Field's Point West of this Light, the shore is quite bold. The course from Fuller's Rock Light to the Light on Sassafras Point is NW. ¾ N., distance ⅝ of a mile. You will pass one red buoy on this last course. From this Light to the city the course is N. by W. The buoys are very prominent all the way up this bay and river, and strangers should be particular to observe the color, and their line of bearings, as the water is quite shoal each side of the channel in many places.

WICKFORD.

Wickford is now quite an important point of railroad communication, therefore yachtsmen will frequent it quite often. If bound there from Newport, when off the North end of Conanicut Island, steer W. ½ N., passing the beacon on the South end of White Rocks on your starboard hand, and a black buoy on James Ledge on your port; continue on about

the same course, and anchor a little North of the black buoy
that lies NE. of Poplar Point Light. If you wish to run in
for the Light from down the bay, bring Poplar Point Light to
bear NW. by W., and run for it, keeping it on your port bow.
Give the point NE. of the Light a good berth.

Directions for East Greenwich.—When Warwick Light bears
North, distance ⅔ of a mile, steer NW. ¼ W., distance 1¼
miles, to a black buoy; from this steer W.NW., distance 1½
miles, to a black buoy on Sally Rock. (If you vary from
these courses, let it be to the Northward, and nothing South of
this line.) After passing the buoy on Sally Rock, steer W.
by S. ¾ S., distance ¾ of a mile, to a red buoy; leave that on
your starboard hand, and continue the course to a black buoy
off Long Point, distance ¾ of a mile; after passing this point,
you will steer about South past a red buoy.

SAUGHKONNET RIVER.

This river will be found a very convenient place of refuge,
and a good harbor for any wind.—From ¼ to ½ a mile West
of West Island (which is the extreme point on the East side
of the river), steer N. ½ E., and as you get up into the river,
keep the West shore little best aboard until up to Fog-Land
Point, which is on the East side, distance 7 miles North of
West Island. Above this point you will have a good harbor,
and below it, for some distance, good anchorage.

In entering this river care must be taken that the point on
the West side of the entrance does not bear East of North, as
there are other shoals in the vicinity of Cormorant Rock,
which you must leave on your port hand, and not approach
near it, only on the East and North sides of it. This rock
bears from West Island NW. by W. ¾ W., distance 2¾ miles.

West Island bears from *Brenton's Reef Light Ship* E. ½ S.,
distance 8 miles.

3

ENTRANCE TO VINEYARD SOUND AND BUZZARD'S BAY.

Gay Head Light bears from the S.E. Point Block Island Light E. ¾ N., distance 34½ miles, and from *Brenten's Reef Light Ship* E. by S. ¾ S., distance 25 miles. *The Sow and Pigs, or Vineyard Sound Light Ship*, bears from Block Island North Point Light E. ¾ N., distance 28⅛ miles, and from Point Judith Light E. ½ S., distance 22¼ miles. *The Hen and Chickens Light Ship* bears from Point Judith E. ¼ N., distance 21½ miles, and from *Brenten's Reef Light Ship* it bears E. ½ S., distance 16⅛ miles. *The Vineyard Sound Light Ship* bears from *Brenten's Reef Light Ship* E. by S. ½ S., distance 17⅝ miles.

The Light Ship off Davis South Shoal bears from Point Judith about SE. by E. ¼ E., distance 80 miles; this course from Point Judith will carry you just South of No Man's Land. *This Light Ship* bears from Sankyty Head Light S. ¼ E., distance 22 miles.

Sailing Directions for Westport Harbor.—When one-fourth of a mile West of the Spindle on Hen and Chickens Reef, steer N.W. by N. ¼ N. You will first pass the red buoy on Lumber Rock on your starboard hand; it is distant from the Spindle 1⅛ miles; you will next make the black buoy that is South of the Two Mile Rock, and distant from Lumber Rock buoy 1⅝ miles; when near this black buoy, keep off to the Northward, and bring the Rock that is at the mouth of the River to bear NW., when you will run for it, passing the red buoy on Half Mile Shoal on your starboard hand, and passing the entrance Rock about 150 to 200 feet on your port hand; keep off the port shore about that distance until to the H. S. buoy on the Middle Ground, and if bound to Westport, pass it on your port hand.

If from the Westward, make the Two Mile Rock buoy (black), pass it on your port, and observe the directions given.

Note this: Do not get within one-fourth of a mile of the Two Mile Rock buoy (black), when NE. of it.

To pass over the Hen and Chickens Shoal North of the Spindle one mile. Steer from Lumber Rock buoy E. ½ N., and you will carry from 8 to 10 feet at low water. This course will bring you just South of Mishaum Ledge buoy, distant from Lumber Rock 4 miles.

CUTTYHUNK HARBOR.

This is a good place of refuge with the wind from any quarter but from N.NE. to E.NE. To enter this Harbor from the Westward, bring the NE. Point of Cuttyhunk Island to bear from S.SE. to E. by N., and run for it until within one-eighth of a mile of the Point, when you will keep about East, passing North of a red buoy that bears E. by N. from the Point. This is Whale Rock buoy; NW. by N. from this buoy is a black buoy on the Middle Ground; this passage is between the two.

Little East of Whale Rock is a buoy on Edwards Rock, H.S. You will leave that on your starboard hand, then steer about S. by E., until past the red buoy on Pease. Ledge, when you will have good anchorage in from 2 to 4 fathoms of water.

Another direction is to run pretty close to the SW. part of Penikese Island, and steer S.SE. ½ E., passing the Middle Ground black buoy on your starboard hand a good berth, and the Middle Ledge buoy on your port; the latter is an H. S. buoy. Gull Island Ledge, a black buoy, bears from this H. S. buoy E. by N. ½ N. When coming in here from the Eastward, you only have to pass between the NW. Point of Nashawena Island and the buoy off the South end of Gull Island, then steer about SW. ½ W.; there is good beating room, and plenty of water.

BUZZARD'S BAY AND NEW BEDFORD.

When the *Hen and Chickens Light Ship* bears NW. by N., distance 2½ miles, and *Sow and Pigs Light Ship* bears S. by W. ½ W., distance 1½ miles, the course to Wings Neck Light is NE. ½ E., distance 21⅝ miles. This course, if made good, carries clear of all Ledges and Shoals to above Wings Point

Light. Pass this Light on your starboard hand, and continue on the above course until you are up to a black buoy, passing it on your port hand. If bound up the Bay any farther, it will be best to anchor near this buoy for a pilot. You will pass Bird Island Light on this course; it bears from Wings Neck W. ½ S., distance 2⅜ miles.

Cuttyhunk Light bears from Wings Neck Light SW., distance 18 miles.

If bound into Sippican Harbor, get Bird Island Light to bear NE. by N., distance ¾ of a mile, then steer N. by W. ½ W., distance 2¾ miles; you will pass black buoy No. 1 on your port hand, and when you get to black buoy No. 3, it will be well to get a pilot.

If bound into Wareham; after passing Bird Island Light one mile, it bearing W. ½ N., steer N. ½ W. up to the Northeast side of Great Hill; distance from the Light, 1½ miles. From this to the town a good pilot is needed.

NEW BEDFORD HARBOR.

The Dumpling Rock Light bears from the *Hen and Chickens Light Ship* NE. ¼ E., distance 7½ miles. Mishaum Ledge is on this line of bearing about midway between the two Lights. (Least water on this ledge is 8 feet.) Therefore, when running for Dumpling Light from near the *Light Ship* do not keep to the North of N.E. by E. the first three or four miles. From the buoy on this ledge you can keep directly for Dumpling Light, and only give it a berth of 300 or 400 feet. You will pass a red buoy on your starboard hand that is on a sand shoal about South from the Light, distance ½ a mile. There is also a black buoy just South of the Light, near to it. When to the Dumpling Light, steer NE. by N., distance 2¼ miles, or until Clark's Point Light bears North, when you will steer N. by E. ¾ E. toward a red buoy on Egg Island Flats, and little South of a black buoy that is on Butler's Flats, which you will pass on your port hand, and then steer N.NW., leaving the red buoy and the beacon on

Egg Island Flats on your starboard hand; on this course you will first pass a black buoy that is nearly a mile from the Butler's Flat buoy; then little North of this you will pass between a red and a black buoy; from these the course is about North, on which you will pass a red buoy, then the black buoy that is close to Palmer's Island Light, which you leave on your port. The best place to anchor is just North of the ferry landing.

Direction No. 2 for New Bedford Harbor.—From the *Hen and Chickens Light Ship* steer NE. by E. ½ E., until Clark's Point Light bears North, when it will be in range with Palmer's Island Light; keep the Lights on this bearing (North) until within about one mile of Clark's Point, when you will observe the first direction.

Direction No. 3.—Steer the course given above from the *Light Ship* until Clark's Point Light bears NW. by N. ½ N., then keep it on this bearing until within one-half mile of it, when you will observe the first directions given.

As the ledges are quite numerous off New Bedford Harbor, I will give the position of the principal ones that will need be passed in entering the harbor.

Wilkes' Ledge H. S. buoy bears from Dumpling Light S. ½ E., distance 1¼ miles. (Ten feet the least water on this ledge.) Great Ledge bears from Clark's Point Light S. ½ W., distance 3¼ miles, and E. ½ S., distance one mile from Dumpling Light; there is a black buoy on the East and a red buoy on the West side of this ledge. (Least depth of water 7 feet.)

Decatur Rock, Church Rock, and Phinny Rock buoys, all bear nearly S. ¼ E. from Clark's Point. The first, Decatur Rock buoy, is red, distance 1⅞ miles; Church Rock buoy lies little South of this, and is red; Phinny Rock buoy is black; distance from the Light 2¾ miles.

North Ledge buoy (black) bears from Clark's Point S. by E. ½ E., distance 3⅛ miles.

Mosher Ledge buoy (red) bears from Clark's Point SE. ½ E., distance 2½ miles. Henrietta Rock buoy (H. S.) is on the same bearing, distance 1¾ miles from the Light   Packet Rock buoy (black) bears from the Light SE. ½ E., distance 1½ miles.

Quick's Hole Passage bears from Clark's Point Light S. ¼ E., distance 8½ miles. Directly off this passage, in Buzzard's Bay, distance ¾ of a mile from the land, there is a Lone Rock buoy; there is 8 feet of water on this rock. By keeping Gay Head Light open East of the SE. point of Nashawena Island, you will pass the East side of this rock.

There is no obstruction in this passage except a ledge on the East side, about midway of each entrance; there is a buoy (red) on this ledge. If you steer South on the first half of the passage, and SE. ½ E. after passing the buoy, you will go all clear. S. by E. is the only straight course through here. The flood-tide runs through here from Buzzard's Bay into the Vineyard Sound.

THE RELATIVE BEARINGS AND DISTANCES OF THE LIGHTS IN VINEYARD SOUND AND NANTUCKET SHOALS.

These bearings must not be mistaken for sailing directions.— Gay Head bears from Montauk Point Light E. by N., distance 48½ miles. From the west end of Cuttyhunk Island to *Pollock Rip Light Ship* by the Ship Channel, the distance is 49 miles.

Gay Head Light bears from the *Sow and Pigs Light Ship* SE. by E. ½ E., distance 7 miles, and from Cuttyhunk Light SE. ¼ S., distance 6½ miles. Tarpaulin Cove Light bears from Gay Head NE. by N., distance 8½ miles; the West End of No Man's Land bears from Gay Head S. ½ W., distance 5¼ miles. Nobska Point Light bears from Tarpaulin Cove E.NE., distance 5¾ miles. Holmes' Hole, or West Chop Light, bears from Tarpaulin Cove E. ¼ S., distance 7⅛ miles, and from Nobska Light it bears SE. ½ S., distance 3¼ miles. East Chop Light bears from West Chop SE. by E. ¼ E., distance 1½ miles.

Succonnessett Shoal Light Ship bears from Nobska Light E. ¼ S., distance 10 miles, and from West Chop Light E. by N. ¼ N., distance 8⅛ miles, and from Cape Poge Light it bears N. by E. ¼ E., distance 7 miles. *Cross Rip Light Ship* bears from Holmes' Hole Light E. by S. ½ S., distance 14 miles, and from Cape Poge Light it bears E. ¼ N., distance 7½ miles. Cape Poge bears from East Chop Light SE. ½ E., distance 6 miles, and from Nobska Light SE. ¼ E., distance 10¾ miles.

Nantucket Harbor, or Brant Point Light, bears from *Cross Rip Light Ship* SE. by S. ¼ S., distance 12¾ miles; the *Handkerchief Light Ship* bears from *Cross Rip* E. ¼ N., distance 10¾ miles; Nantucket Great Point Light bears from *Cross Rip* SE. by E. ¼ E., distance 11½ miles, and from *Handkerchief Light Ship* S. ½ W., distance 5¾ miles; *Butler's Hole Light Ship* bears from the *Handkerchief* NE. by E. ¼ E., distance 4 miles; *Butler's Hole* bears from Nantucket Point Light N.NE. ¼ E., distance 9 miles; *Pollock Rip Light Ship* bears from *Butler's Hole* E. by S. ½ S., distance 8½ miles, and from Nantucket Point it bears NE., distance 10 miles; Monomoy Point Light bears from *Butler's Hole Light Ship* N. ¾ E., distance 1¼ miles; *Pollock Rip Light Ship* bears from Monomoy Light SE. ¾ E., distance 3¾ miles; Chatham Lights (two) bear from *Pollock Rip* N. ½ E., distance 8 miles; Sankaty Head Light bears from *Pollock Rip Light Ship* S. by W. ¾ W., distance 15 miles.

The Bishop and Clerks' Light is 4⅛ miles S. by E. from Hyannis Light; it bears from *Cross Rip Light Ship* N.NE. ¼ E., distance 7¾ miles, and from *Handkerchief Light Ship* NW. ½ W., distance 9½ miles; *Succonnessett Light Ship* bears from it W. ½ S., distance 8½ miles.

Directions for Entering Hyannis Harbor from the Westward.—Steer past Nobska Light E. by N. ¾ N., distance from it from one-half to one mile, until *Succonnessett Shoal Light Ship* bears E. ¾ S., distance about 6 miles, when you will run for it on your port bow, passing it on that hand; when about one mile East of it, steer E. by N. ¾ N. about 6 miles, when Hyannis Light will bear N. by E. ½ E., distance 2¾ miles; then run for it on that bearing until the East end of the Breakwater bears W. by N., then haul up about N.NW. or N. by W., and you will find good anchorage in three fathoms of water. When you haul up N. by E. ½ E. for the Light, you should have the buoy on W.SW. Ledge on your port, and be pretty near it; this is a bell buoy in summer and spar buoy in winter; it lies in the range of the East end of the Breakwater and Hyannis Light. This direction will take you North of L'Homme Dieu Shoal.

Another direction that will take you between L'Homme Dieu and Hedge Fence Shoals is, to get Nobska Light to bear W. ¾ N., then steer E. ¾ S., keeping it directly over your stern until *Succonnessett Light Ship* bears NE. ¾ E., then steer E. by N. ¾ N., and observe other directions. On this course you should pass a black buoy on Eldridge's Shoal on your starboard hand. It bears from the *Light Ship* SE. by E. ½ E., distance ⅞ of a mile.

If bound to Hyannis from the Eastward, steer from the *Handkerchief Light Ship* NW. ¼ W. toward the Bishop and Clerk Light, passing it on your port hand, distance ⅜ of a mile; continue on this course until Hyannis Light bears N. by E. ½ E., then as before directed.

A proper attention must be given to the current when on these courses across the tide.

Directions for Entering Edgartown Harbor.—When off the Oak Bluff Dock ¼ to ⅓ of a mile, steer SE. ½ E., or directly for Cape Poge Light (you will be South of Squash Meadow Shoal on this bearing). When Edgartown Light bears SW. ¾ S. you will steer S.SW. until the Light bears West; you will then gradually haul toward it, passing the red buoy off the Light on your starboard hand. When in past the Light, the shore on the port is quite bold until around the point. There is good anchorage W. by S. from the Light. Care must be taken when coming from the Westward, and not let Cape Poge Light bear East of SE. by E. until you get Edgartown Light to bear SW. ¾ S.

When coming from the Eastward, steer from *Cross Rip Light Ship* W. ½ N., keeping it bearing E. ½ S. until Cape Poge Light bears S. ¼ E., when Edgartown Light will bear SW.; then run in for it on this bearing until Cape Poge bears E., when you will keep the Light open more on your starboard bow to pass the Point buoy; the course in after passing this buoy is W. by N. If beating into Edgartown, tack ship when the bottom changes from sticky to hard.

Directions for Nantucket Harbor.—If from the Westward, when East of *Cross Rip Light Ship*, steer SE. ½ E., distance 5½ miles, to clear the East end of Tuckernuck Shoal, on which there is a buoy; from this steer S. by E. ½ E., distance 6 miles, to the bell buoy.

I will here give the Coast Survey directions for entering the harbor; but a careful attention to the Black and Red buoys will be as sure as any direction aside from them, as the buoys are changed to suit the channel; keeping as in all cases the Black on the port, and the Red on the starboard, going into a harbor.

There are two small pyramidal wooden structures, 300 feet apart, NW. and SE. and NW. by W. ½ W. from Brant Point Light. The following are correct guides for entering the harbor of Nantucket in 1876: Bring the Cliff Beacon Lights (red and white) in range, and run for them, passing near the bell buoy in 3 fathoms water; keep on this course until up with the Red Buoy No. 2 on the outer bar (the course on this range is SW. ½ S.); then steer for Brant Point Light S. by E., passing the red buoys Nos. 4 and 6; then for Red Cliff beacon light SW. by S. ½ S. until the rear beacon and Brant Point Lights are in range; then steer on this range, passing the red buoys (outer, middle, and inner black, flat buoys Nos. 8, 10, and 12). The course on this range will be SE. by S. ½ S., passing Brant Point within 100 fathoms, and steer SW. for the anchorage in from 2 to 3 fathoms, soft bottom.

IN VINEYARD SOUND AND OVER NANTUCKET SHOALS.

The main part of the flood tide sets to the Eastward, and the ebb to the Westward. In steering courses that run much North or South of East and West, careful attention should be paid to the direction of the current and the wind.

At *Pollock Rip Light Ship* the tide changes from East to Westward 2½ hours before South Moon, and at Holmes' Hole a little before South Moon; thus a South Moon brings it about high water in the Vineyard Sound and on the Shoals. The flood tide runs through Quick's Hole from Buzzard's Bay into the Vineyard Sound about S. by E.; ebb the opposite direction.

Sailing Directions for Vineyard Sound and Nantucket Shoals.—When the *Vineyard Sound Light Ship* bears N. by W., distance 1¾ miles, and Cuttyhunk Light bears N.NE., distance about 3 miles, steer E. by N. ¼ N., you will pass about 3 miles North of Gay Head, and one mile South of Tarpaulin Cove Light on this course. When Nobska Light bears NW. by W., steer SE. by E. about 5 miles, or until West Chop, or Vineyard Haven Light, bears W. by N. ½ N.; when you will steer E. by S. ½ S., for *Cross Rip Light Ship* distance 14 miles from West Chop. Cape Poge Light should be passed about 4 miles distant on this course. After passing *Cross Rip Light Ship* two miles on the above course, steer E. ¼ N., to the *Handkerchief Light Ship*, distance from this point 8¾ miles; when past the *Handkerchief*, steer NE. by E. ¼ E., for the *Shovelfull or Butler's Hole Light Ship*, distance 4 miles, passing her on the port hand; then haul to E. by S. ½ S. for *Pollock Rip Light Ship*, distance 3½ miles; if you wish to pass out by the ship channel, pass the *Light Ship* on your port hand, and continue on this course until you pass a red buoy on your port, and an H. S. buoy on your starboard hand, distance from the *Light Ship* 2 miles. Chatham

Lights should bear N. by W. ½ W., when you will be clear of the broken parts of Pollock Rip.

If you wish to pass through the Northern Slue, when to the *Light Ship* pass her on your starboard hand, and steer NE. by N. ¼ N.; this will take you through in 3 fathoms at low tide. There is a buoy bearing North from the *Light*, distance one-half a mile, and one N.NE. from the *Light Ship*, both of them to be passed on your port hand; but the one that is N.NE. from the *Light Ship* should be passed close by.

Chatham Lights bear N. ¼ E. from *Pollock Rip Light Ship*, distance 8 miles.

VINEYARD HAVEN.

In entering this harbor, give the middle ground shoal a good berth, and the point off the West Chop Light; there is a red buoy on the point East of the Light, distance ⅜ of a mile. The buoy on the East end of the middle ground bears from the Light NW., distance nearly ½ a mile. The shoal extends about 5 miles from this buoy W. by S., with water on it varying from 2 feet to 15; the shoalest part is near the East end. There is a good passage South of the middle ground shoal.

LONG DISTANCES AND COURSES FROM POLLOCK RIP LIGHT SHIP OFF MONOMOY POINT.

From Pollock Rip Light to Cape Elizabeth Lights, near Portland, the distance is 120 miles, course NE. by N. ½ N. for 8½ miles until Chatham Lights bear West, then N. ½ E. to Cape Elizabeth. From Pollock Rip to Manheigan Island the course is NE. by N. ¾ N., distance 136 miles.

From Pollock Rip to Mount Desert Rock Light NE. ¼ N., distance 165 miles. Machias Seal Islands bear from Pollock Rip NE. ½ E., distance 215 miles. This Island lies W.SW., distance 11 miles from the West end of Grand Menan Island.

From Pollock Rip to the Seal Islands, off the SW. end of Nova Scotia, the course is E. by N. ½ N., distance 203 miles.

It is not expected that either a sailing craft or steamer can make this a sure run, as the tides and winds vary the course so much. I give these as their relative position.

COURSES, BEARINGS, AND DISTANCES FROM POLLOCK RIP TO MASSACHUSETTS AND BOSTON BAYS, WITH SOME SAILING DIRECTIONS.

If bound to Boston, the course from *Pollock Rip Light Ship*, is NE. by N. ½ N. 8½ miles, when Chatham Lights (two) will bear West, then the course is N. ½ E., distance 11¼ miles, when Nauset Lights (three) will bear West, then N. by W., distance 14 miles; the Highland Cape Cod Light will then bear SW., the course from here to Boston Light is NW. by W. ¼ W., distance 40 miles.

If you wish to go into Provincetown Harbor, when Race Point Light bears SW., then haul up W. by S. until it bears East ¾ of a mile distance, then run S.SE. ¼ E. until Cape Cod Light opens south of Wood End Light, or Wood End Light bears E. ½ N. 1¼ miles distance, then run E. by S. ½ S. until Race Point Light opens Northeast of this Light, or this Light bears NW. by N., then run NE. by E. ½ E. until Long Point Light bears NW. ⅜ of a mile distance, then run North until Wood End is in range with it, or it bears SW. by W. ½ W., then run W. by N., and anchor in 4 to 8 fathoms with Wood End Light bearing SW. by S. ¼ S., and Long Point Light bearing SE. ¾ E.; there is a fogbell here. At Long Point there is a bell, and on Race Point a steam fog whistle, and a Daboll fog trumpet at the Highland Light, as described in the Index.

PLYMOUTH, KINGSTON, AND DUXBURY.

If you are bound to Plymouth, Kingston, or Duxbury, when Race Point Light bears SW., steer W. ¾ S., distance 19 miles, to Gurnet Point Lights; then follow these directions: These Lighthouses consist of two octagonal wooden towers, 31 feet apart, ranging NW. and SE., and serve as a range to clear Brown's Bank, coming from Southward and Eastward, and as a guide into Plymouth Harbor, Kingston, and Duxbury. In coming from the Northward bound to Plymouth, you must not bring the Lights to bear South of S. by W. to clear High Pine Ledge, which lies about 2½ miles North of the Gurnet; off this ledge there is a spar-buoy (red No. 6). When in the channel abreast of these Lights, run up W. ½ S. for Duxbury Pier Light, and leave it on the starboard hand in running in.

From South and East, bring Gurnet Lights in range until Duxbury Pier Light bears W. ½ S., when you will be midway between the Lights and the nun buoy on Brown's Island Shoal; then steer W. by S. until Duxbury Pier bears W. by N., when you will be midway between red buoy No. 6 and black buoy No. 5; then steer W. ½ N., pass between red buoy No. 8 and black buoy No. 7, leaving Duxbury Pier Light one-half cable's length on starboard hand; then steer North and anchor under the lee of Muscle Bank, in from 5 to 8 fathoms of water, or continue on same course between red buoy No. 10 and black buoy No. 9, and anchor in the Cow-Yard, in from 4 to 5 fathoms water. This is a good harbor for vessels overtaken in Easterly storms. Depth of water in channel at low tide, 18 feet.

BARNSTABLE.

If bound to Barnstable, after you are West of Race Point steer S. by W., distance 18½ miles, up near the buoy off the bar: when coming in, bring Sandy Neck Light to bear SW. by S. ½ S., and steer for it, passing close to Bar buoy (red No. 2); then SW. by W. ¼ W., for black buoy No. 1, leaving it on the port hand; then for the Light, rounding the Point, giving it a berth of half a cable's length. There is 7 feet of water on the bar at low tide. Anchorage near Light in 3 fathoms of water.

WELLFLEET.

If you wish to go to Wellfleet from off Race Point, steer S. by E. until Billingsgate Island Light bears E. by N. ½ N., distance 4½ miles, and Sandy Neck Light bears SW. by W. ½ W., nearly 9 miles; then you will be at or near Billingsgate Shoal; from this haul up East, and the first buoy is

nearly 5 miles distant, or to the Light, bearing S. by E.   The
buoys or a pilot must then be depended on, it being quite a
shoal-water harbor.

BOSTON BAY AND HARBOR.

Minot's Ledge Light bears from Boston Light S.E. ¼ E., distance 7 miles; the bell buoy off Hardin's Ledge bears from
Boston Light SW. ¼ S., distance 2½ miles.

Directions to Enter Boston Harbor.—When running in for
Boston Light, keep it within the bearings of NW. by W. to
W. ½ N.; this will give Hardin's Ledge on the port a good berth,
and will clear the Egg, or Shag Rocks on the starboard hand.

Keep Boston Light well on the starboard bow, passing South
of it one-half a mile, and when it bears North, steer W. ½ N.,
passing Nash's Rock buoy on the starboard hand (this buoy
bears from Boston Light SW., distance ⅔ of a mile); continue
on this course until Long Island Head Light opens West of
the Narrows Light (red); you will then gradually haul up
for this Beacon Light (a screw-pile structure), passing close
by it on your starboard hand; then steer NW. ½ W. until
to the East end of Gallup Island, which will be right ahead
on this course; from this point steer NW. by W. until Long
Island Head Light is in range with the Beacon or Nick's Mate,
or it bearing West; you will then slowly work up to W. by
N., passing midway of Long Island Head and the beacon on
Deer Island Point; from this steer W. by North for Castle
Island, or Fort Independence; when up to black buoy No. 7,
or between that and red buoy No. 8, steer NW. ½ N., passing
the black buoy No. 9 on your port; from this buoy the course
to Long Wharf is NW. ½ W.

There is an automatic whistling buoy off the Graves, in
place of the bell buoy formerly there.   It bears from Boston
Light NE. by N., distance 2¾ miles.

If you should make this buoy in a fog, or at night, from
one-eighth of a mile East of it, steer South until Boston Light

bears W. ½ N., before hauling in for it; or bring it in range with Long Island Head Light, and run in for it. These bearings will take you clear of Shag Rocks.

The Graves buoy bears from Egg Rock Light S. by E., distance 4 miles.

There is good anchorage to the Westward of Long Island Head Light.

When going in past Boston Light, you can pass within one-eighth of a mile of it if you like (leaving Nash's Rock buoy on your port hand); then steer West one mile to red buoy No. 6, when you will keep the Narrows Light on your starboard bow, and observe the other directions.

The Narrows Light bears from Boston Light about *West*, distance 1⅜ miles.

Long Island Head Light bears from the Narrows Light NW. by W. ¾ W. distance 1¾ miles. This bearing is right over Gallup Island. The buoys on the Centurion bear from Boston Light W. by S. ¾ S., distance 1⅛ miles, and from the Narrows Light they bear SE. ¾ S., distance ⅜ of a mile. It is hardly necessary to give the buoys in detail as they are passed; by following the courses given, it will be very plain work to follow the channel by observing the position and color of the buoys as you make them.

The beacon off Point Allerton bears from Boston Light S. by E., distance ⅞ of a mile · there is a black buoy outside of the beacon. This beacon bears from Harding's Ledge bell buoy W.NW., distance 1¾ miles.

If running for Boston, Salem, Marblehead, or Gloucester Harbors, and overtaken by the fog, do not get into less than twenty fathoms of water, but if you find yourself in less water than that, steer East until you deepen it, as this course will take you clear of everything anywhere in Boston Bay, if near to the twenty fathom line.

BOSTON HARBOR FROM BROAD SOUND.

After passing Egg Rock Light, and Nahant Head, work in to the Westward, and get the Narrows Light (Red) to bear S. by W. ¾ W. Egg Island Light will be directly over your stern, when heading for the *Narrows* Light on this bearing, which you will keep on until Long Island Head Light bears W. by S. ¾ S., distance 2 miles, when you will be to or very near the black buoy No. 3, that is on the West side of Aldridge's Ledge. From near this buoy the course to steer is W. by S.; keeping Long Island Light on the port bow, and as you approach it, pass midway of it and the Deer Island beacon. On this last (W. by S.) course, you will pass the black buoy (No. 5) that is on the Ram Head Shoals. When you are to Long Island Head, observe the other directions given.

The above directions will take you in as good water as that passage affords.

To Enter Nantasket Roads.—When up to Boston Light, and it bearing North, distance ⅔ of a mile, steer W. ½ S., which will bring you near to the buoys on the Centurion; pass these on your starboard hand, then steer W.SW. until Long Island Light opens clear of the SW. part of George's Island, then haul up toward that Light and run in for the anchorage anywhere to the Westward of Fort Warren, which is on George's Island.

HINGHAM HARBOR.

After you pass the Centurion buoys, steer SW. by W. until you open the passage between Hull and Paddock's Island, you will then haul in and pass between the two, keeping little nearer to the land on the port hand; then steer S. by E. ¼ E. toward a black buoy which you will leave on your port hand; from this buoy steer SE. by S. ½ S. toward the West end of Bumkin Island, distant from this buoy three-eighths of a mile; passing this island on your port, you will continue on about the same course, and pass between a red and a black buoy, but you should haul around near to the red one, and steer South by East for Crow Point, which is distant from the red buoy nearly three-fourths of a mile. After passing Crow Point, let your course come little more to the Eastward, and when Chandler's Island bears North, and Sailors' Island South, it will be as well to hold on for a pilot.

QUINCY OR WEYMOUTH.

When you are between Paddock's Island and Hull (or Nantasket), steer S. by W. until Pig Rock Beacon bears SW. ½ W., when you will steer for it until between Prince's Head on the starboard, and Sheep Island on your port hand ; then run S. by E. ½ E. until the West end of Sheep Island bears NE. ½ N. ; you will then steer SW. ½ S., passing between a red and a black buoy, distance from the island 1½ miles. This is a good place to hold on for a pilot.

Another Direction to Get to this Place.—When Fort Warren, or George's Island, bears North ¼ of a mile, steer SW. ¾ W., toward a red buoy that lies W. by S. ¼ S., distance ½ mile from the West end of Paddock Island ; when near to this buoy, steer SE. ¾ E., making a little curve to the Southward, and passing Pig Rock Beacon on your starboard hand ; then keep toward Sheep Island, and observe the directions given above.

Boston Bay, and Eastward.—Cape Ann, or Thatcher Island Lights, bears from Boston Light NE. ¼ E., distance 23 miles.

From the Highlands, or Cape Cod Light, they bear N. ¾ W., distance 41 miles.

Eastern Point Light bears from Long Island Head Light NE. ½ E., distance about 19½ miles.

Directions for Marblehead Harbor.—Halfway Rock bears from Marblehead Light E. by S. ¾ S., distance 2⅝ miles. (There is a beacon on this rock.)

After passing this rock, which you leave some distance on your starboard hand, bring Marblehead Light to bear W. by N. ½ N., and run for it, passing Marblehead Rock on your port hand, and when it (the rock) bears SW., steer NW. until the Light bears S. by W., then steer SW. ½ W. into the harbor.

4

Salem Harbor.—When coming from the Southward, bring Baker's Island Lights to bear NW., then bring the low Light in sight little East of the high Light, and run for it.

This will take you to the Eastward of the Southeast breakers, outer breakers, and Searl's Rock. Give Baker's Island a wide berth, leaving it on the port hand, and bring Hospital Point Light to bear from W. by N. ½ N. to W. by N. ¾ N., and run for it. This course will take you up channel between Misery Ledge and Bowditch Beacon.

When Fort Pickering Light is in range with the Light on Derby's wharf up the harbor (they bearing SW. by W. ½ W.), then run in and find good anchorage SW. by S. from Fort P. Light, and Derby's Wharf Light, bearing W. by S.

The Hospital Point Light at Beverly has a lens placed in the line of the center of the main ship channel, making a more brilliant fixed Light on that line than on either side of it, and serves as a guide to vessels in mid-channel, clear of dangers on either side.

The Southeast Breaker, which is the outermost ledge from Baker's Island, has on it a red buoy. It bears from Baker's Island Lights SE. by S. ½ S., distance nearly one mile, and from Halfway Rock it bears NE. ¾ E., distance ½ mile.

You can run in for Baker's Island Lights with them bearing from NW. to W. by S.

FOR GLOUCESTER OR CAPE ANN HARBOR.

When coming from the Eastward, bound into Gloucester Harbor, give Eastern Point Light a good berth to clear. Eastern Point Ledge, near which is a spar buoy (red No. 2), which bears from the Light SW. ¾ S., ¼ of a mile distant; when near this buoy or the Light bears NE. ¾ N., run NW. ½ N., until Ten Pound Island Light bears N.NE. ½ E., then run for it until Eastern Point Light bears E.SE. (good anchorage here), or run NE. by E. ¾ E. to the inner harbor.

Ten Pound Island Light bears from Eastern Point N. by E., distance 1⅜ miles. Cape Ann Light bears from Eastern Point NE. by E. ¼ E., distance 5¼ miles.

From the North Cape Ann Light, the East part of the Dry Salvages bear N.NE., distance 2 miles; Straitsmouth Island Light bears from the North Cape Ann Light N. by W., distance 1⅝ miles. The structure is a white octagonal tower, lantern black, with a plank walk over the rocks toward a one-story white dwelling. This is a local light for Rockport, and the channel inside, or West of the Dry Salvages, which you leave on your starboard hand when bound into Rockport, or into Ipswich Bay. The Dry Salvages, and the Flat Ground, bears from Straitsmouth Light from E. by N. ¼ N. to N.NE., distance 1 mile; therefore this Light must not be approached within those bearings at night.

There is a passage more than one-fourth of a mile wide between the Large Salvage Rock and the Flat Ground, which has a red buoy on the South end of it. Avery's Rock buoy (red) bears from this Flat Ground buoy SW. ¼ S., distance 1¼ miles. Avery Rock has only 6 feet of water on it, and lies East of the buoy. It bears from Straitsmouth Light N. by E. ½ E., distance nearly ¾ of a mile.

The Londener Rock bears from Cape Ann Lights SE. by E., distance ½ a mile. There is a good passage between the Lights (or Thatcher's Island) and the Londener, on which there is a Spindle. There is a good passage for small vessels North of Thatcher's Island, but you should keep the island the best aboard.

WHITE ISLAND LIGHT.

White Island Light (one of the Isle of Shoals) bears from Cape Ann Lights N. ½ E., distance 20 miles; Whale Rock Light, at the mouth of Portsmouth Harbor, bears from White Island Light N. by W. ¾ W., distance 6½ miles.

On Cape Neddick, near York River, Me., there is a light to be established; this cape bears from Boon Island Light NW. ¼

W., distance 6 miles, and from White Island N. by E. ¾ E. distance 12 miles.

Boon Island bears from White Island NE. ¼ E., distance 12 miles.

Newburyport Harbor Lights bear from White Island SW. ¾ W., distance 12 miles, and from Straitsmouth Island Light they bear NW. by N., distance 13½ miles.

The Newburyport Lights are in range for crossing the bar in the best water, and as there are constant changes of the channel, and the water quite shoal, I will only advise taking a pilot to enter the Merrimack River.

THE ISLE OF SHOALS.

White Island, on which the Lighthouse is situated, is the Southwestern Island of the group. There is only one obstruction in running for or to this Light, within the bearings of NE. ¾ E. to W. ½ S. (by the Southward), except Anderson's Ledge, which bears from the Light SE. by E. ½ E., distance nearly 1 mile. You can approach the Light East of it, close aboard, and on the West side, within ⅜ of a mile.

The South shore of Star Island bears from White Island Light NE. by E. ½ E., distance little more than ½ of a mile. The West side of Lunging Island, *i. e.*, Square Rock, bears from the West Ledge of White Island N. ½ E., distance ½ a mile.

To Enter Gosport Harbor.—Bring White Island Light to bear S.SE., distance one mile, then steer E. by S. ½ S., distance one mile, and you will be in from 5 to 8 fathoms of water (low tide) between Smuttynose Island and Star Island, and NW. of Cedar Island. Hog Island, or Appledore, the largest of the group, bears from this harbor N.NW.

When coming from the Northward, give Appledore a little berth on your port hand, and enter the harbor steering SE. There is a passage between Appledore and Smuttynose by steering W. ½ S., keeping Smuttynose best aboard.

You can enter the harbor by passing White Island Light on your port hand close to it (distance ⅛ of a mile), then steer N. ½ E., leaving the Half Way Rocks buoy on your starboard hand. If the buoy is not seen, keep close to the SE. part of Lunging Island, and when past the island, you can haul to E. by S. for the harbor. If in a craft not drawing more than 5 or 6 feet of water, you can enter this harbor by passing between Star and Cedar Islands, keeping midway of the two. At high water, there is from 12 to 14 feet of water in this passage.

Cedar Ledge bears from the Light E. ½ N., distance 1¼ miles, and from this passage between Star and Cedar Island E.SE. ½ E., distance nearly ½ a mile.

Duck Island, and the Ledges surrounding it, bears from the Light from NE. ½ N. to N.NE. ¼ E., distance 2⅜ miles; and from Appledore Island to the middle of Duck Island, NE. ½ N., distance ⅞ of a mile. There is good sailing room between Appledore and Duck Islands, but give the latter a good berth.

SAILING DIRECTIONS FOR PORTSMOUTH.

When coming from the Westward bring the Light on the Isle of Shoals, *i. e.*, White Island Light, to bear East, distance 1½ miles, then steer N. ¾ W. Or you can bring Whale's Back Light to bear N. ¾ E., distance ⅞ of a mile, when Portsmouth Light will bear N. ¾ W., distance 1¾ miles; you will run for it on this bearing until past Whale's Back Light. On this run you will pass Kitt's Rock buoy, about ⅜ of a mile on your starboard hand; it bears from Whale's Back S. by E. ¾ E., distance ⅓ of a mile. When past Whale's Back Light, steer about N. ½ E., keeping Portsmouth Light on the port bow, passing it on that hand, and after you are well past the Light, haul gradually to W. ¼ N. for Fort Washington, and when you are where you can see the two South Ship Houses past the point of Seavy's Island (which is opposite Ft. Washington), haul up to N.NW. ¼ W., and you will pass on your port a Bk. buoy and a beacon; then you can haul toward the docks.

When approaching Portsmouth Harbor from the Eastward at night, bring Portsmouth Light to bear NW. ¾ W., and run for it until White Island Light bears SW. by S., when you will steer W.NW. until Portsmouth Light bears N. ¾ W., then you will be on the other directions given.

If you run in here for a *harbor* you will find good anchorage with Portsmouth Light bearing from S. by E. to SE. ½ E., distance from ¼ to ⅜ of a mile.

Between Whale's Back and Portsmouth Lights you will pass on your port a black buoy on Stielman's Rocks; it bears about South from Portsmouth Light, distance ¼ of a mile. There is a black buoy on Cod Rock that bears from this Light N.NW., distance little more than ⅛ of a mile, and NE. ½ N., distance ⅜ of a mile from the Light. There is a red buoy off Fishing Islands.

Gunboat Shoal bears from Whale's Back Light S. by W., distance 2⅓ miles; there are 4 fathoms of water on this shoal. Whale's Back bears from White Island Light N.NW. ¼ N., distance 6¼ miles.

Boon Island Light bears from White Island, or Isle of Shoals, NE. ½ E., distance 12 miles, and from Cape Ann Lights it bears N.NE., distance 29 miles.

Cape Elizabeth Lights bear from Cape Ann NE. by N. ½ N., distance 57 miles.

Monhegan Island Light bears from Cape Ann NE. ½ E., distance 87 miles.

Pemaquid Point Light bears from Monhegan Island Light NW. ½ W., distance 9½ miles.

Matinicus Rock Light, off Penobscot Bay, bears from Cape Ann NE. by E. ¼ E., distance 102 miles.

Mount Desert Rock Light bears from Cape Ann E. by N. ¼ N., distance 133 miles.

From Mount Desert Rock Light to Machias Seal Island the course is E. by N. ¾ N., distance 54 miles.

This course from Cape Ann to Monhegan Island will carry you in sight of Boon Island Light, also of Seguin Island Light. The course given for Matinicus Island from Cape Ann carries you in sight of Monhegan Island Light.

The course to Mount Desert Rock Light carries you in sight of Matinicus Island Light.

I do not propose to enter into a detail of all harbors and places of refuge on the coast of Maine, as it is not the purpose I had in view, neither could a small work of reference, as this is intended to be, do the subject the justice it demands.

In running for Cape Elizabeth from near the Isle of Shoals, it is as safe to run the North side of Boon Island one mile or so, on account of Boon Island Ledge, that lies E. ¾ S., distance 3 miles from the Light. There is a first-class Nun buoy on this Ledge.

York Ledge will be passed on your port hand ; it bears from Boon Island Light W. ¾ S., distance 5 miles. There is an iron spindle on this Ledge.

Cape Porpoise Light bears from Boon Island N.NE., distance 14 miles. Wood Island Light bears from Boon Island N.NE. ¾ E., distance 20 miles. Cape Elizabeth bears from Boon Island NE. ¾ N., distance 28 miles, and from Wood Island Light NE. by E., distance 8½ miles.

SAILING DIRECTIONS FOR PORTLAND HARBOR.

When coming from the Westward, if at night, do not approach within three and one-half or four miles of Cape Elizabeth Lights, on account of the East and West Hue and Cry Rocks, which bear from the Lights SE. ¾ S., distance 3¼ miles. There is a black can buoy off the Southern part of these rocks. The Alden Rock and Corwin Rocks Buoys bear from this buoy about North, distance 1¾ miles, and from Cape Elizabeth

Lights SE. by E. $\frac{1}{4}$ E., distance $2\frac{1}{4}$ miles. There is only six feet of water on Alden's Rock.

Keep outside of these dangers, and bring Portland Head Light to bear NW. by N., and steer for it on that bearing until within one-third of a mile of it, when you will keep up past it close aboard on your port hand, then steer N. by W. until to the black buoy off Spring Point, which you will pass on your port hand, and then steer NW. $\frac{1}{2}$ W. until to another black buoy off the Breakwater Light; you will haul around that buoy, keeping nearer to the City side of the Harbor.

When running for Portland Harbor, if you should make one of these outside reef buoys at night, it would be best to pass South of it, as the reefs mostly lie to the Northward of the buoys. Give the H. S. buoys a good berth on either hand.

There is an automatic signal whistling buoy, placed about one-half a mile to the Southward of Old Anthony Rock Buoy, which is an H. S. can. If you can make this signal buoy at night, run for it if to the Westward of it, and pass it close aboard on either hand, and steer NE. by N. until you get Portland Light to bear NW. by N., then proceed as before directed.

This will take you to the Northward of the outside ledges.

Old Anthony Rock Buoy bears from the Hue and Cry Buoy NW. by W., distance $1\frac{1}{2}$ miles, and from Alden's Rock Buoy, W.SW. distance $1\frac{3}{8}$ miles.

Directions to Enter the Harbor North of these Rocks.—Haul well in toward Richmond Island, and when to the black buoy on Watts' Ledge (which buoy bears from Cape Elizabeth Lights SW. $\frac{1}{2}$ S., distance $1\frac{1}{2}$ miles), steer NE. until Portland Head Light bears NW. by N., when you will steer for it, and observe the above directions.

On this course from Watts' Ledge Buoy, you will pass

Taylor's Reef black buoy on your starboard hand, you will give it a good berth, as the buoy is on the South part of the reef. You can pass the Lights within one-eighth of a mile of the shore.

Old Anthony Rock H. S. buoy bears from Watts' Ledge buoy E. by S. ¼ S., distance 1¾ miles, and from Cape Elizabeth Lights S. by E. ¼ E., distance 1⅝ miles.

Directions for Portland from the Eastward.—When close in to Half Way Rock Light, bring Portland Head Light to bear West, and run for it, and you will pass Witch Rock buoy on your starboard hand, distance ¼ of a mile, and little less than that distance South of Ram Island Ledge. When one-half a mile of Portland Light, steer NW. ½ N. until past the buoy off the SW. point of Bang's Island. Then see other directions.

Bulwark Rock, on which there is 14 feet of water, bears from Portland Head Light E.SE., distance 5½ miles, and from Half Way Rock Light SW. by S., distance 4 miles.

Jordan's Reef buoy, H. S., bears from Portland Light SE. ½ E., distance 1 mile.

KENNEBEC RIVER.

If from the Westward, when Halfway Rock Light bears North, distance 5 miles, steer NE. by E. ½ E. for Seguin Island Light until within one-fourth of a mile of it, when you will haul up N. by E. until Pond Island Light bears N. ¼ W., then steer about for it on your port bow, keeping it a little open as you approach the river. If the wind is strong from the northward, and you want to keep to the windward, you can go about one mile NW. of Seguin Light, passing just South of the Jackknife Ledge and Pond Island Bar buoys. This buoy on Pond Island bar, you leave on your port hand as you keep up for the river. It bears from Pond Island Light about South, distance ⅜ of a mile.

If bound into the Kennebec from the Eastward, bring Seguin

Island Light to bear W. ¾ N., and run for it until Pond Island
Light bears NW. ½ W., distance nearly 3 miles, then steer
for it on this bearing until into the mouth of the river. On
this last course (NW. ½ W.) you will pass Tom's Rock buoy
on your starboard, and a black buoy on White's Ledge on
your port hand. White's Ledge buoy bears from Pond Island
Light SE. ¼ S., distance 1 mile.

There is good anchorage NE. by E. from Pond Island Light,
and East of Stage Island.

To proceed up the river when East of Pond Island Light
(close by it), steer N. ½ E. until you pass the spindle on the
South Sugar Loaf, which you will leave on your port hand.
The course then is NW. to the south point of Long Island.
This spindle is distant from Pond Island three-eighths of a
mile, and the South end of Long Island is distant from the
spindle nearly three-fourths of a mile. The North Sugar
Loaf is one-fourth of a mile above the spindle.

After passing the South end of Long Island, the course
is N. ¼ E., passing close by Cox Head on your port hand, and
to an H. S. buoy below Perkins Island; leave this buoy on
your starboard, and when it is East of you, the course
is N. by E. ½ E. to a black buoy opposite the North end
of this Island; leave this buoy on your port hand, and
steer N. by E., distance 1¼ miles, to Bald Head (which
is North of the entrance to Back River). When up to this
Point, steer NW. by N. about one mile, you will pass a spindle on your port hand on this run; when you come to this
turn of the river, haul gradually to about N.NE., passing a
spindle on your port, then Pettis Rocks on your starboard
hand; N.NE. ¾ E., distant three-fourths of a mile above
this spindle, there is another spindle on the North end of Ram
Island. You will leave this on your starboard hand. There
is a good passage East of these rocks and Ram Island.

From Ram Island Spindle to the buoy on Lithgow's Ledge,
the general course is N. by E. ½ E., distance 2¼ miles. This
should be an H. S. buoy.

From Ram Island Spindle to Lincoln Ledge, distance 4 miles, there is no obstruction except Lithgow's Ledge, if you keep near the middle of the river, or the West side best aboard.

Lincoln's Ledge is seven-eighths of a mile above Fiddler's Reach; the course through here is W.NW., then haul up to N. ¾ E., passing Lincoln Ledge and Trufant Ledge buoys on your port hand.

The distance from Pond Island Light to Bath is 11 nautical miles.

Directions for Entering Ebencook Harbor.—This harbor is on the Northwest end of Southport Island, East side of the entrance to Sheepscot River.

Bring Seguin Island Light to bear W. ¾ N., distance 2½ miles, when you can steer N. by E. ½ E. for Hendrick's Head Light, which is nearly 7 miles distant from this bearing of Seguin. When you are past Tom's Rock, which bears from Seguin NE. by E. ¾ E., distance 2¾ miles, and the Sisters, that bear from Seguin NE. ¾ E., distance 2⅝ miles, you can bring Hendrick's Head Light within the bearings of NE. by N. ½ N. to N. ¾ E. This last bearing will take you pretty near the Cat Ledges; they bear S. ½ W. from Hendrick's Head Light, distance 1¼ miles.

When you are up to these Ledges, keep the Light well open on your starboard bow, to clear the Cedar Bush Ledge that lies S. ½ W., distance ¼ of a mile from the Light. When up to the Light, if near to it, steer N. by E. ½ E. until the entrance to the harbor opens south of Green Island; this will clear a shoal spot of 16 feet, that is N. by E. ¾ E., distance ⅝ of a mile from the Light, and ¼ of a mile from the shore. When the harbor entrance opens, you will steer about E. by S. until past the point of Green Island, then keep most any course you please North of East, and choose your anchorage.

Bull's Ledge buoy, H. S., bears from Hendrick's Head Light N. by W. ¼ W., distance nearly ⅞ of a mile. Eight feet is the least water on this Ledge.

Griffith Head Ledge bears from Hendrick's Head Light SW. by S., distance 2½ miles; this is an H. S. buoy. Least water 7 feet.

When running for Seguin Island Light on the bearing given above, i. e., W. ¾ N., do not get North of that, until past Bantam Rock, which bears East from the Light, distance about 6 miles, and from the South end of Damiscove Island it bears SW. by S. ½ S., distance 1⅝ miles.

Directions to Enter Booth Bay Harbor.—When Seguin Island Light bears W. ¾ N. anywhere from 2 to 5 miles distant, you will steer for the beacon on the Cuckolds, passing it on your port hand; when this beacon bears West from you, distance ¼ of a mile, steer N. by E. ½ E. directly for Burnt Island Light, passing West of Squirrel Island. Burnt Island is distant from the Cuckolds Beacon 2¾ miles. When up to Burnt Island, steer about N. by E., distance about ¾ of a mile, when you will gradually haul to NE. by E. into the East Harbor, or Town's End; or you can haul to N.NW., and anchor in West Harbor.

If bound into *Booth Bay from the Eastward*, bring Pemaquid Point Light to bear North, distant 1½ miles, when you can steer W. ¾ N., directly for the South end of Squirrel Island.

You will pass the Hypocrite Islands and Fisherman's Island on your port, and the Gangway Ledge buoy on your starboard hand.

When about one-half a mile from Squirrel Island, or Burnt Island Light bears NW. by N. ½ N., you can haul up for it, passing East of Squirrel Island; you will then observe the first directions.

DIRECTIONS FOR ENTERING JOHN'S BAY AND RIVER.

Bring Pemaquid Point Light to bear North, and run for it until within one-half mile of it, when you will haul to W. by N., distance ¾ of a mile to about South of Pemaquid Point, which bears SW. by W. ½ W., distance one-half mile from the Light. When you open the bay past this point, steer N. ¾ W. for John's Island, passing it on your starboard hand, and when West of it, (if close to it,) steer North, passing Thurston's Lodge, which is ⅜ of a mile North of John's Island on your starboard, and McFarlin's Ledge that is ⅜ of a mile NW. ¼ N. from John's Island on your port hand. After passing this Ledge keep up near the middle of the river. There is good anchorage on either hand, as you get up to where the river widens.

If you want to stop in *McFarlin's Cove,* when you are just to the North end of Beaver Island (a small island little North of John's), you can steer W. ½ N., passing close by Davis Island, where you will have good anchorage in 4 to 6 fathoms of water.

There is also a good harbor East of Beaver Island which you can enter by hauling around North of the island. There is a passage into it East of John's Island, and both sides of Knowles' Rock, but not very wide.

When running for Pemaquid Light from the Southward, it will not do to let it bear East of NE. ½ N., until well in to it, on account of Pemaquid Ledge, which bears from the Light SW. ¼ S., distance 1¼ miles; there is 16 feet of water on it.

Pemaquid Point Light bears from Monhegan Island Light NW. ¼ N., distance 9½ miles.

There is a Whistling Signal Buoy near the Duck P cks; it bears from Monhegan Light N.NW. ¼ N., distance 1 mile.

Sailing Directions for St. George's River.—When coming from the Westward, bring Monhegan Light to bear South,

distance 2 miles, and steer NE. $\frac{1}{2}$ N., for the SE. part of
Burnt Island, which is 4$\frac{1}{2}$ miles distant from this bearing of
Monhegan.   When to Burnt Island, you will haul up around
it within $\frac{1}{8}$ or $\frac{1}{4}$ of a mile, then steer N. $\frac{3}{4}$ E., until you
make a red buoy on the Sisters; you will pass it on your
starboard hand, and when North of it, steer N. $\frac{1}{4}$ E., or
directly for the SE. point of Teals Island, distant from the
Sisters buoy 1$\frac{1}{4}$ miles; when about one-eighth of a mile of
this Island, steer NE. $\frac{1}{2}$ E., toward Hooper's Point, 1$\frac{1}{8}$ miles
distant.

There is an H. S. buoy on Channel Rock, one-quarter of a
mile W. by N. from this point; you can pass it on either
hand, then steer N. $\frac{3}{4}$ W. until the main part of the river
opens to view, so that you can haul up to NE. $\frac{1}{2}$ E.; there
are no obstructions, only near the shores, until above the
Narrows, when you will see a black buoy on Bailey's Ledge;
pass this on your port hand, then keep up about NE. by E.,
or midway of the shores to St. George's Fort, where I will
leave you.

*Another Direction to Enter St. George's River, when West of
Monhegan Island.*—Run in East of Pemaquid Point Light,
and bring Franklin Island Light to bear within E.NE. to
NE. by E., and run for it, passing it close aboard on your
starboard hand.   (Franklin Island Light bears from Pema-
quid Light E. by N. $\frac{1}{2}$ N., distance 6$\frac{3}{4}$ miles, and from Monhegan Island Light N. $\frac{1}{2}$ W., distance 8 miles.)   When you
are past Franklin Island Light, steer NE. by E. $\frac{1}{2}$ E., and
you will pass on your starboard hand a red buoy on Jenks'
Ledge, distance from the Light 3 miles; then seven-eighths
of a mile farther in, you will pass on your port hand an
H. S. buoy on Goose Ledge, next a Bk. buoy on the same
hand.   You will then be in the line of other directions given.

*Directions to Enter Herring Gut Harbor from the West-
ward.*—You will observe the first directions given for St.
George's River until you are one-eighth of a mile above the
red buoy on the Sisters.   (This buoy is distant 1$\frac{3}{4}$ miles, N. by

E. ¼ E. from Burnt Island.) You will then keep directly for Marshall's Point Light, steering E. by N. ¾ N., passing on your starboard hand a red buoy, which is distant from the Light three-eighths of a mile ; and when past this buoy, haul up to NE. ½ N., and keep about midway of the shores, until up to the harbor.

Another Direction to Enter Herring Gut is to steer about NE. past Burnt Island and Old Cilley Ledge, until Marshall's Point Light bears N. ¾ W., when you will run about for it, passing close to Gunning Rocks ; they bear about S. by E. ¼ E. from the Light, distance ⅝ of a mile. From these Rocks keep the Light open on your starboard hand, and keep up to the harbor, as before directed.

To Enter Herring Gut from the Eastward.—When close to the SW. point of Mosquito Island, steer NW. by W. ½ W., until you are near a buoy, which you pass on your right, then run about West, passing another buoy on the same hand, when you can haul up around Marshall's Point Light. Keep the middle of the river to the harbor.

There is no obstruction in the way of running in for Burnt Island from just East of Monhegan, to Burnt Island bearing NW. ½ N. Burnt Island has the appearance of being nearly round, and is about ⅝ of a mile in diameter. Mosquito Island has about the same appearance, and is one-half a mile in diameter. It bears from Burnt Island NE. by E., distance 4 miles. Both of these are the outermost islands of the shore group, and when running along the coast near to them, keep a little SE. of their line of bearings, and you will be clear of these ledges, *i. e.*, the Old Man's Ledge, that bears SW. by W., distance 2 miles from Burnt Island, and Old Cilly Ledge, that bears NE. by E., distance 2 miles from Burnt Island.

It is best to keep within two miles of the line of these two islands, and you will be all clear of the Roaring Bull, Hooper's Shoal, and Metinic Ledge. They lie about NE. and SW.

from one another, and their extreme distance apart is 2⅝ miles. This course is *North* of them.

Directions to Enter Tennant Harbor.—You can bring Tennant's Harbor Light to bear anywhere from N.NE. to W.NW. when to the Northward of Metinic and Green Islands, and run for it open on your port bow, passing it on that hand, and when the Light bears South, distance ⅛ of a mile, steer W. by N. ½ N. for a black buoy which you will leave on your port hand. You will have good anchorage just above this buoy.

Tennant's Harbor Light bears from White Head Light W. ¾ S., distance 2⅞ miles.

Sailing Directions to Enter Penobscot Bay through Two Bush Channel.—Run in for White Head Light with it bearing NE. by E., and when Tennant's Harbor Light bears NW. by W. ¾ W., run directly from it on that bearing, steering SE. by E. ¾ E., distance about 3 miles, when White Head Light will bear NW. ¾ N. If it is flood-tide care must be taken not to drift on to Crow Island Ledges, which extend off one mile SW. from the land. When you get White Head on this bearing, haul up directly to NE. ½ E., and run on this course about 4 or 5 miles, when you will gradually haul up to N. by E. ½ E., and keep that course until Owl's Head opens North of Munroe Island, when you can haul up toward it, or shape the course for your destination. I give this direction to work on at night, as I do not advise the Muscle Ridge only by daylight.

Tennant's Harbor Light bears from the Northern triangles NW. by W. ¼ W., distance 6⅜ miles. These triangles bear from White Head Light SE. ¾ S., distance 4½ miles.

To enter the bay through Two Bush Channel at daylight, when you are to Metinic Island Ledge, steer E.NE.

This ledge bears W. by N. from the North end of Metinic Island, distance nearly 2 miles, and has on it an H. S. spar

buoy placed on the SW. part of the Ledge.   Give it a berth of
½ a mile if you go to the Eastward of it.   Least water 7 feet.

You can run in for the bay from SE. of Metinic Island
by bringing White Head Light to bear North, and run for it
until to the South Breaker, which bears South from White
Head Light, distance ⅝ of a mile.

On this course you will pass between the shoal ground off
the East side of Metinic Island and the Southern Triangles,
which are sometimes *Bare* and always *Break*.   You will not
find less than 4 fathoms of water off the East side of Metinic
Island ; the shallowest spot is about ¾ of a mile from the shore
opposite the middle of the island.

The West part of the Southern triangles bears from White
Head Light S. ¾ E., distance 5½ miles.

*To Enter the Penobscot Bay from one-half to three-fourths of
a mile South of Monhegan Island Light.*—From this position
steer E. by N., and it will take you to the North end of Matinicus Island.   This island lies North of Matinicus Rock
Light, distance about 5 miles.   On this course you will pass
about 2 miles North of Bantam Ledge buoy spar (H. S.).   It
bears from Matinicus Light NW. ½ N., distance 5 miles.
You can pass either side of this buoy, distance 200 feet.
When you are about 1½ or 2 miles distant from Matinicus
Island, steer N. ½ W. into the bay, and when Owl's Head
Light opens North of Munroe Island, or it bears N.NW. ½ W.,
you can run for it open on your port.

To Enter Penobscot Bay from the Eastward.—You will bring
Saddleback Ledge Lights to bear within the bearings of NW.
¾ W. to N. ½ E., and run for it until it is distant 1½ miles,
when you will steer W. by N. ½ N. until Heron Neck Light
bears E.NE., then steer NW. by N. ½ N. for Owl's Head Light.

On this run as here given from off Saddleback Light, to the
Bay, you will pass the Bay Ledge buoy (a red can) on your
port hand at some distance ; you can sail around this buoy
by giving it a berth of one-half a mile.

5

Saddleback Ledge Light is about 17 miles E. ½ S. from White Head Light.

PENOBSCOT BAY FROM WHITE HEAD LIGHT TO BELFAST
AND CASTINE; INCLUDING THE HARBORS OF
ROCKLAND, ROCKPORT, CAMDEN AND
FOX ISLAND THOROUGHFARE.

Sailing Directions for Muscle Ridge Channel.—From North of Monhegan Island, distance 2 miles, steer NE. by E., or for White Head Light on the bearing of NE. ½ E., and as you draw near to it, keep it pretty close aboard on your port hand, that you may pass inside or North of the South Breakers, which has on it a red buoy and a bell buoy. Keep on this NE. by E. course, passing first a red spindle that is on Yellow Ledge, it bears from the Light East, distance over ⅝ of a mile; leave this on your starboard hand, and the next buoy is a black one that is on Hay Island Ledge, distance from the Light little less than ½ a mile. You will then make a horizontal striped buoy on Inner Gangway Ledge, which you will leave on your port hand. (But you can pass it on either hand.)

From this buoy, or little East of it, steer NE. ¼ E. for 3¾ miles, passing the following marks in the order given:

First on your starboard hand is an H. S. buoy on Hurricane Ledge, distance from the Gangway buoy ⅜ of a mile; next is a black buoy on Sunken Ledge, which you leave on your port hand, distance from the last buoy ⅜ of a mile; then a spindle on Garden Island Ledge, which you leave on your port, and about one mile above this you will pass on the same hand a spindle on Otter Ledge.

Above this spindle ⅜ of a mile there is a black buoy on Ash Island Ledge, and about East of that is an H. S. buoy on Upper Gangway Ledge; on the course given you should pass between the two. You can pass this H. S. buoy on your port if necessary, and you will have on your starboard a red buoy that is on Inner Grindstone Ledge. The next mark is the beacon on the East side of Ash Island; when this bears West from ¼ to ½ of a mile distant, to go into Owl's Head Bay, steer N.NE. ½ E. toward a red buoy on Sheep Island Bar, distance from the beacon 1¾ miles.

On this run you will pass on your starboard hand an H. S. buoy that is on NW. Ledge; it is distant from the beacon just one mile. After passing Sheep Island buoy on your starboard hand, steer NE. ¼ N., passing on your port a spindle that is on Dodge's Point, continuing the course out of the Bay; and if bound up the West side toward Belfast, steer N.NE. ¾ E., distance 12 miles, when Grindel Point Light will bear E.SE. You will then keep up the Bay about N.NE. or N. by E., keeping nearer to the West shore. When Belfast Bay opens, haul gradually into it, passing Steel's Ledge on your starboard hand, then keep about in the middle of the passage to the town. Steel's Ledge has a beacon also a buoy on each end. It is about six miles from Grindel Point Light to Belfast Bay.

We will end our directions here, and return to Owl's Head Light. Then if you are bound up the Bay by the East passage to Castine, you will steer from near the Light E.NE. for five miles, to clear McIntosh Ledge, then keep NE., which will take you to Upper Mark Island, distance from Owl's Head 13¼ miles; you will pass this Island on your starboard hand, then steer NE. by N. ½ N. for Dice's Head Light, distance 7½ miles from Mark Island.

Directions to Enter Castine Harbor.—Bring Dice's Head Light to bear N.NE., distance ½ a mile, then steer E. by N. ½ N., passing on your port a black buoy on Otter Rock Shoal off Fort Point; then further in, a stone beacon on Hosmer's Ledge; you will leave this on your starboard hand. Northeast of this beacon, distance ½ a mile, is a red buoy on the NW. end of the Middle Ground; pass this on your starboard hand if you wish to go above the town.

You will find good anchorage in Lawrence Bay, which you can enter by getting the middle of the town at the docks to

bear NW., and steer SE., working around to South as you
enter the Bay. You will have from 3 to 4 fathoms of water.

The water outside of this Bay is quite deep all around
Castine.

*From Muscle Ridge Channel out through Fisherman's Island
Channel.*—When the beacon on Ash Island bears West, distance ⅛ to ¼ of a mile, steer E.NE., passing on your starboard
hand a red buoy on Grindstone Ledge, and on your port a
black buoy on Sheep Island Shoals; continue the course
about 2¾ miles, or until Owl's Head Light opens North of
Munroe Island, or it bears N.NW. ½ W., when you can keep
for the Light if bound up the West side, and if bound up the
East side of the bay, a NE. course will take you to Upper
Mark Island.

There is another passage out of the Muscle Ridge Channel,
which is, to haul around close to the North side of Otter
Island, and steer E. ½ S. if it is flood-tide, but on the ebb,
steer E. ¼ N. The tide runs very strong through these channels, and a careful attention must be paid to the direction it
runs.

*Muscle Ridge Channel Buoys that can be passed on either
hand.*—First—the Lower Gangway Ledge H. S. buoy. This
buoy is placed on the West side of the ledge, which is quite
small. Second—Hurricane Island Ledge is a red buoy placed
on the West side of the ledge; you can pass it on the port
hand *if necessary*, but do not get more than ¼ of a mile East
of it. West of it you can stand close in to the land; if possible, keep this side of it. Third—Garden Island spindle.
This ledge is about ⅛ of a mile long, North and South. Do
not get within ⅜ of a mile of this spindle NE. of it, as there
is a shoal spot with 12 feet of water on it near that position.
Fourth—Otter Island Ledge spindle, with plenty of water
either side of it. Fifth—Upper Gangway Ledge H. S. buoy;
both sides of this there are red and black buoys to mark the
passage. Sixth—The NW. Ledge H. S. buoy. If bound

through Owl's Head Bay, pass this buoy on your starboard hand.

SEAL HARBOR.

To enter Seal Harbor, which is only ½ a mile North of White Head Light, when up to Hay Island Ledge black buoy, haul around it on your port hand, and steer N.NW. until to a red buoy on your starboard, and a black buoy on your port hand, where you will have good anchorage. To enter from the Northward, give Burnt Island Ledge black buoy a good berth in rounding it.

ROCKLAND HARBOR.

From North of Owl's Head Light ½ a mile, steer W. by N. and you will pass on your port hand a black buoy on Spear's Rock, then a red buoy on your starboard hand that is on the South end of South Ledge; when West of this buoy run for any part of the town if the tide is up.

If from the Northward, haul around South of the red buoy off Jameson's Point, and steer W.SW., passing on your starboard hand an H. S. buoy on Jameson's Ledge, and on your port a black buoy that is on the North end of North Ledge.

Mean rise and fall of the tide in this harbor 9 ft. 6 in.

ROCKPORT HARBOR.

From Owl's Head Light bearing South ½ a mile, steer North 4 miles, and after passing North of Rockland Harbor, you will first pass a black buoy on your port hand that is on Ram Island Point; then one mile above this, a beacon on Porterfield Ledge, which you will leave on your starboard hand.

You can sail all around this beacon to the spindle on Lowel Rock, which is South of Indian Island Light.

When this Light bears East ¼ of a mile distant, steer N. ¼ E., passing two red spindles on your starboard hand, and a stone beacon on your port; then keep midway of the shores.

Porterfield Ledge, or outer-Rockport beacon, bears from Indian Island Light S. by W. ¼ W., distance ⅝ of a mile.

CAMDEN HARBOR.

From ¼ of a mile East of Owl's Head Light steer N. by E., or for Negro Island Light on that bearing, and you will pass Indian Island Light, distance ⅝ of a mile, on your port, and ⅞ of a mile above that, you will pass the Graves on your starboard hand, distance ½ a mile. As you approach Negro Island Light keep it open on your port, passing it on that hand, and a red buoy on your starboard, which lies ¼ of a mile NE. ½ E. from the Light; you will then steer N.NW. into the harbor. You can enter this harbor from the Northward by hauling around close to the spindle on NE. or Morse's Point, leaving the black buoy and the spindle on Outer and Inner Ledges on your port hand. This passage is narrow, but you will have 3½ fathoms of water by keeping near to the Point.

There is a beacon on the Graves, and it bears from Negro Island Light S. by E. ¼ E., distance 1¼ miles, and from Indian Island Light NE. by E. ½ E., distance 1½ miles. Mean rise and fall of tides, 9 ft. 8 in.

SAILING DIRECTIONS FOR FOX ISLAND THOROUGHFARE.

Brown's Head Light is on the South side of the entrance to the Thoroughfare, and bears from Owl's Head Light E. ¼ S., distance 6 miles.

To enter the Thoroughfare, bring Brown's Head Light to bear E. by N. ½ N., and run for it on that bearing, keeping it on your port bow until you are East of Drunkard's Ledge spindle, and Fiddler's Ledge beacon, both of which you pass on your port hand. You will pass Dogfish spindle on your starboard hand. It bears from Fiddler's Ledge beacon SE. ½ S., distance ½ a mile.

Do not attempt to pass Dogfish spindle on your port hand when going in, as it is very rocky South of it.

Drunkard's Ledge spindle bears from Fiddler's Ledge beacon W. by N. ½ N., distance ⅝ of a mile.

Fiddler's Ledge beacon bears from Brown's Head Light W. by S., distance 1½ miles.

Dogfish Ledge spindle bears from Brown's Head Light SW. by W., distance 1¼ miles; but note this: you must not approach the Light on that bearing when SW. of the spindle, on account of the Inner Bay ledges, the North end of which bears from the light SW. by W. ¾ W., distance 2⅝ miles.

There is a red buoy on the North end of the ledge, and a red one on the South end, ⅝ of a mile apart, bearing S. by W. from each other.

When you are in past these dangers, bound into Fox Island Thoroughfare, keep Brown's Head Light on your starboard hand, passing the Sugar Loaf Islands on your port, steering about NE., and you will first pass a spindle on Fox Ears; second, an H. S. buoy on Calderwood Ledge; then a black buoy on Cross Island Ledge; all of these on your port hand. You will then keep about midway of the land, and observe the character of the buoys as you make them, which I will name in the order as passed for a distance of five miles from the Cross Island Ledge buoy.

First, an H. S. buoy on Post Office Ledge, distance 1⅜ miles; 2d, a black buoy on Lobster Ledge, distance ¼ of a mile from the last; 3d, a black buoy on Grindstone Ledge, distance from the last black buoy ⅜ of a mile. You will pass all of these on your port hand, when you will be near a spindle on Iron Point Ledge; pass this close at hand on your starboard, then steer NE. by E. ½ E., passing first an H. S. buoy on Waterman's Ledge, then a Black buoy on Fish Point Ledge, both on your port hand, and from near the last buoy steer E. by S. ¾ S., passing a spindle on Goose Rocks on your port, and Widow's Island on your starboard hand. You will see Channel Rock ahead on your starboard bow, but it is best to pass it on your port hand, on account of Black Ledge buoy, which bears about East of this rock. This ends the Thoroughfare and brings you into Isle Haut Bay, for which I am not prepared to give any direction.

Southern Harbor is North of the entrance to Fox Island Thoroughfare, and to enter it observe the first directions given for this passage, until Brown's Head Light bears E. by N. ½ N. or Fiddler's Ledge beacon bears West ½ a mile, when you will steer NE. ½ N. for Amsbury Point, distance 2 miles, passing the Sugar Loaves on your starboard hand. You can pass Amsbury Point on your port and keep up into the harbor, or you will have good anchorage near to it on either hand.

Directions for Entering Burnt Coat Harbor.—This harbor is on Swan Island; it bears from Mt. Desert Rock Light NW. ½ N., distance 17 miles, and from Matinicus Rock Light NE. ¾ E., distance 27½ miles. This is a good place of refuge, and can accommodate a large number of vessels. There are two Lights on Swan Island, and to enter the harbor bring them in range, when they will bear NE. ¾ N.; then run for them in range until you are pretty close to them, when you will steer E. by N. into the harbor.

When running in for the Lights in range, you will first pass Heron Island Ledge buoy on your port hand; it is distant 3 miles SW. ¼ S. from the main Light. You will next leave Harbor Island on your starboard hand. The West point of this Island bears from the Light S.SW. ½ W., distance ½ a mile. You will also pass Harbor Island Ledge on your starboard hand. The passage between the Ledge and the Light is about ¼ of a mile wide. There is a Wrought Iron spindle on this ledge which you only need give a berth of 100 feet.

SAILING DIRECTIONS FOR MOUNT DESERT ISLAND HARBORS.

After passing Matinicus Rock Light, if near to it, steer NE. by E. ½ E., keeping South of all the islands, and when Baker's Island Light bears NE. ½ N., distance 7 miles, Mt. Desert Rock Light will bear S. by E. ¾ E., distance 11 miles. You will then steer N. by E. until near Bunker's Ledge spindle (red); this spindle bears from Baker's Island Light W. ¼ N., distance 3¾ miles. There is a black buoy off the Nubble, or Long Ledge, that bears from Bunker's Ledge buoy about West, distance ⅝ of a mile.

.On this N. by E. course you will pass the Little and Great Duck Islands on your port hand. After you have passed between these buoys steer NE. ¾ N., distance ⅞ cf a mile, passing first a red buoy on your starboard, then a black one on your port, when you will steer N. by E., or for the East end of Greening's Island ; on this course there is a bar with 1¼ feet of water on it. If bound into Southwest Harbor, when it opens to view steer NW. by W. ; there is no obstruction until near the head of the harbor.

If you wish to go to *Bar Harbor* from here, when SW. Harbor opens and the NW. point of Great Cranberry Island bears SE. (Cranberry Island is the land on your starboard hand up this passage), then steer E. ½ S. until past Bunker's East Ledge, on which there is a beacon ; or you can keep for Bear Island Light until past the West end of Sutton's Island, when you will steer East, passing two red buoys on your port hand and North of Bunker's Ledge, and a black buoy on Lewes Rock that is just North of the ledge. After this it is only necessary to give the island a good berth.

When running up the East side you will pass a little island, the Thrumbcap, that lies ⅛ of a mile from the shore, then the Round Porcupine, which you leave on your starboard hand ; give the land a little berth on your port hand as you haul around into Bar Harbor. Do not attempt to go in beyond the steamboat wharf, or you may find bottom if the tide is up, ' as the bar will be under water.

This direction given for *Southwest Harbor* will do very well by daylight, but if you wish to enter in the night, when you make Baker's Island Light steer for it open on your port bow, and as you approach it give it a good berth, and when it bears West, distance ½ of a mile, steer N. ½ W. nearly 2 miles, or until Bear Island Light bears NW. by W. ½ W., when you will keep it on that bearing and run for it, passing between Bunker's Ledge Beacon and Sutton's Island. You should on this course be about ¼ of a mile South of the ledge, and ⅛ of a mile from the island when you pass them. As you approach Bear Island

Light keep working off to the Westward until you are heading
W. by S., and when past the East end of Greening's Island a
W. by N. course will take you into the harbor.   There is a shoal
extending off the SW. part of Greening's Island with a red
buoy on it.

If you are bound to Bar Harbor from Baker's Island, bearing West, ½ mile distant, steer about N.NE., and follow the
island as before directed.

The distance from Baker's Island Light to Bar Harbor is 10
miles.   On this run up the bay you will pass on your right a
Light on Egg Rock; it bears NE. by N. ½ N., distance 8
miles from Baker's Island, and from Bar Harbor SE. ½ S.,
distance 4 miles.

To Enter Bass Harbor, run in on the first directions (*i. e.*,
N. by W.) until Bass Head Light bears NW., when you can
run towards it, passing it about ¼ of a mile distant on your
starboard hand, where you will find the best water over the
bar (from 14 to 15 feet).   When to the Westward of the bar
steer North into the harbor, passing on your port hand the
black buoy on the East end of Weaver's Ledge

Mt. Desert Rock Light bears from Baker's Island Light
S. ¼ W., distance 12 miles.

*Sailing Directions for St. John, N. B., from 1½ miles North
of Mt. Desert Rock Light.*—A NE. by E. ¾ E. course will
take you to Cape Lepreau Light, F. W.   This Light bears
NE. by E. from the North point of Grand Menan Island.   The
following are the principal Lights that will be passed on this
course of 95 miles; and the distance they lie from the line of
that course.   By giving these distances, if you are running
through here in the night you can easily determine if you need
to haul to the North or South, as you approach the Lights.

The first Light passed will be Petit Menan, F. V. W. F.;
it will be 8 miles distant when bearing North.   Second, Mistake Island, or *Moose A Bec* Light, Flg. W., will be distant

4 miles when North. South by West, distance 2 miles from this Light, there is an automatic whistling buoy. Third, Libby Island, F. W., about 4 miles distance when North. Then Machias Seal Islands, two Lights will be passed about 7 miles distant when they bear South. The next is Little River Light, F. V. W. F.; you will pass South of, 2½ or 3 miles distant. Then West Quoddy Head, F. W., will be 3 miles distant when North. You will then pass Grand Menan Island South of you about 5 miles. Then comes the South Wolf Light, Flg. W., which you will pass South of about 2 miles. Then Cape Lepreau Light should be ahead; keep it open on the port bow, and give it a little berth as you approach it.

From off this Light, distant ½ to ¾ of a mile, steer E. by N., distance 17 miles, when Partridge Island Light will bear NW. by N. ¼ N. In steering this course (E. by N.), you should make Cape Spencer Rev. Light on your starboard bow. It bears from Cape Lepreau E. ¼ N., distance 26 miles. After getting Partridge Island Light on the above bearing, steer NE. ½ N. up to a bell buoy that bears E. ½ S. from the Light, distance ⅜ of a mile. You will pass this buoy on your port hand, then steer about N. ½ W., keeping the Light on the point of Carlton Flats on your port, and continue on about the same course.

A careful attention must be paid to the current, when coming into this Harbor, and have plenty of chain over-hauled, as the water is very deep only on the flats.

Mean rise of the tide at St. John is about 23 feet. Time of high water, at full and change of moon, 11h. 21m.

DISTANCES, COURSES, AND BEARINGS,

WITH

SAILING DIRECTIONS,

FROM

NEW YORK SOUTHWARD

TO THE

DELAWARE AND CHESAPEAKE BAYS.

THE HUDSON RIVER,

WITH A FEW COURSES AND DISTANCES IN NAUTICAL
MILES FROM GOVERNOR'S ISLAND.

From Governor's Island to Hoboken, N. ½ E., distance 2¾
miles; from this to Spuyten Devil Creek, N.NE. ¼ E., distance 9¾ miles; from Spuyten Devil to Piermont Dock Light,
course N. by E. ¼ E., distance 10 miles; from thence to
Rockland Lake Landing the course is N. ¼ W., distance 6½
miles; from this to Haverstraw, NW. ½ N., distance 3¾
miles; from Haverstraw to Stony Point Light, course N.NW.,
distance 2⅛ miles; from this Light to Peekskill Dock the
distance is ¾ of a mile; from Peekskill to West Point
Light, distance 8 miles; from West Point Light to Newburgh
is 7 miles; from Newburgh to New Hamburg, distance 5½
miles; New Hamburg to Poughkeepsie, distance 7 miles;
from Poughkeepsie to Hyde Park, distance 4¼ miles; from
this place to Esopus Light, distance 5 miles; from Esopus to
Rondout, distance 3⅜ miles; from Rondout Light to Saugerties Light, distance 9½ miles; from Saugerties to Catskill,
distance 9¼ miles; from Catskill to Hudson City, distance
3¾ miles; from Hudson City to Four-mile Point Light, 3¼
miles; from this to Coxsackie Light, distance 4½ miles;
from Coxsackie Light to Stuyvesant Light, distance 2 miles;
from Stuyvesant to New Baltimore Light, nearly 2½ miles;
from New Baltimore to Cow Island Light, distance 4 miles;
from Cow Island to Albany, distance 7 miles; from Albany
to Troy, 7 miles; making the distance to Albany by river
119½ nautical miles.

ON THE SHORES OF NEW YORK BAY THERE ARE SIX
LIGHTS TO SERVE AS CHANNEL RANGES,
LOCATED AS FOLLOWS:

The Elm Tree and New Dorp Beacon Range Lights are
situated on Staten Island, about three miles SW. from Staten
Island Light; they serve as the Swash Channel Range. Their
line of bearing is NW. ¼ N.   Sandy Hook Point Light bears
from the Shore Light SE. by S. ½ S., distance 6⅝ miles.

The Seaside and Wilson Beacon Range Lights are for the
ship channel from Gedney's Channel to West of SW. Spit.
Their line of bearing is W. by S.   The Shore or front Light
bears from Sandy Hook Point Light W. ¾ S., distance 5⅝
miles; the rear Light is ¾ of a mile inland.

The Conover Beacon and Chapel Hill Range Lights are
for the ship channel from West of SW. Spit up past the
West bank.   The Shore Light of this range bears from the
Hook Point Light SW. ¼ S., distance 3¾ miles; the rear Light
is 1⅜ miles inland.   Their line of bearing is S. by W. ¼ W.

COURSES AND BEARINGS

FROM NEW YORK DOWN THE BAY.

From off the Battery to Robbin's Reef Light the course is
S.SW., distance 3 miles.   From off Robbin's Reef Light steer
S. by E., distance 4 miles, until Staten Island Light bears
NW. by N. 1⅜ miles.   Then the course is S. by W. ¼ W.,
down the ship channel for 7⅛ miles.   If at night, you will
have the Chapel Hill Light in range with the Conover Beacon
Light; keep them in range until the Bayside and the Wilson
Beacon Range Lights bear W. by S., then run on their range
to sea, or E. by N., until Sandy Hook Point Light bears
W.SW., then steer SE. ¼ S., which is the course out on the
Swash Channel Range; or E. by S. ¼ S., out of Gedney's
Channel.

If you wish to go down the Swash Channel, steer as
before given, S. by W. ¼ W., until the Elm Tree Beacon
Light, on the shore of Staten Island, comes in range with
the New Dorp Beacon Light, on the Hill on Staten Island,
when they will bear NW. ¼ N., then steer down SE. ¼ E.,
keeping the high Light a little open North of the shore or
low one.   This carries you to sea, leaving the Stone Beacon
on the port hand.

At Fort Lafayette, on the East side of the entrance to the
Narrows, there is a fog bell station, but no Light.   The
water is deep close in to the Fort.

Directions for Entering New York Bay from the Eastward.
—Pass about 4 miles North of *Sandy Hook Light Ship*, and

bring Sandy Hook Point Light to bear W. by S. ½ S., and run for it on that bearing until it is distant 1½ miles, when you will be on the Swash Channel Range. You can then keep up this range as in other directions given, or you can pass in by the Hook on the Ship Channel Range Lights, steering W. by S. until the Conover and Chapel Hill Range Lights are in line, which will take you up ship channel, from West of Southwest Spit, to the Narrows.

Sailing Directions for Raritan Bay, South Amboy, Perth Amboy, and Tottenville.—Prince's Bay Light is in range with the following marks, which bear from the Light E. by S. ¾ S.: First, the Round Shoal black buoy, which is on the North side of the Shoal, and is to be passed on the port hand when going in through this channel; it is distant from the Light ⅝ of a mile. Second, SW. Spit buoy, distance 8¼ miles. Third, Sandy Hook Point Light, and the P. S. entrance buoy to the South channel, distance from the Hook 2⅜ miles.

When a little inside of the Hook, steer W. by N. ¾ N. for Prince's Bay Light, and as you approach it, keep it open on your port bow, and bring it to bear W. by N., distance ¼ of a mile, when you will steer SW. ¾ S. through the channel for 1⅞ miles, or until the North one of the two entrance buoys bears NW. by W., when, if bound to Perth Amboy or Tottenville, steer for this buoy, passing it on your starboard hand, then work to the Northward, toward Ward's Point, as you enter the river. If bound to South Amboy, when below these buoys keep to the South of the South buoy, and after passing it, steer for the end of the docks at South Amboy.

If from New York, and bound to these places with a free wind, pass close around the black buoy that is just South of Staten Island Light, leaving it on your starboard hand, then steer SW. ¾ S., 6¾ miles, passing South of the red buoy on Old Orchard Shoal, and when Prince's Bay Light bears W. by N. ¾ N., you can follow the first direction given, or change your course to W. ¼ S., and you will pass North of the black buoy that is off Conaskonk Point; from this buoy to the buoys off the entrance of the rivers, the course is W. by N.

You can run for Prince's Bay Light on the bearing of W. ½ N., and it will take you South of Old Orchard Shoal, and close by Seguine Point, which is very bold. Conaskonk Point buoy bears from Prince's Bay Light SE. ¾ S., distance 2¼ miles. If bound up Raritan Bay from New York, and the wind SW., I should advise working down the ship channel until below all the West Bank buoys.

NEW YORK YACHT-CLUB COURSE.

For the benefit of my yachting friends I will write out the relative bearings and distances of the principal objects passed on the Race Course of the New York and Brooklyn Yacht Clubs. Starting from ⅜ of a mile West of Ft. LaFayette or the middle of the Narrows. There are times, when sailing down the bay, that it is difficult, if not impossible, to see from one buoy to another. By observing the bearings and distances I here give, you can govern yourself by them, and not be obliged to get out the chart and rule when time is precious. I will try and make this as plain as possible, so that he who sails may read and understand.

From Ft. LaFayette, bearing East ⅜ of a mile, to the black buoy No. 13, off the Lower Quarantine buildings, the course is S. ¼ W., distance nearly 2⅜ miles; from No. 13 to No. 11 (black), S. ¼ W., distance ¾ of a mile; from No. 11 to No. 9, course S. by W. ¼ W., distance ⅞ of a mile; from No. 9 to No. 7 (black) the course is S. by W. ¼ W., distance 2 miles; Southwest Spit buoy, or No. 8½, bears from No. 7 S. by E. ½ E., distance 1¾ miles. Buoys Nos. 9, 11, and 13, are the West Bank buoys.

We will start again from the same point. From ⅜ of a mile West of Ft. LaFayette to buoy No. 16 (red), the course is S. by E. ¾ E., distance 2¾ miles; this buoy (No. 16) bears from the West end of Coney Island SW. by S. ¼ S., distance ⅝ of a mile; No. 14 (red) bears from No. 16 SW. by S. ¼ S., distance 1⅝ miles; from No. 14 to the horizontal striped buoy (red and black) the course is S.SW., distance nearly 1½ miles. This H. S. buoy is at the point of intersection of the Ship and Swash channels; No. 12 (red) bears from it S. ½ W., distance ⅝ of a mile; SW. Spit (No. 8½) is about on the same bearing, distance from No. 12, 1¾ miles; buoy No. 10 bears from the horizontal striped buoy S. by W., distance 2⅛ miles; and the SW. Spit buoy bears from No. 10 SE. by E. ½ E., distance ⅜ of a mile; Southwest Spit buoy bears from the West end of Coney Island S. by W. ¾ W., distance 6 miles; No. 8 (red) bears from No. 11 (black) S. ¾ E., distance 1⅞ miles; Southwest Spit buoy bears from No. 8 S. by E. ¼ E., distance 2⅝ miles; from the Romer beacon it bears SW. ¾ S., distance 2¼ miles. It should be observed that from South of buoy No. 8 to the SW. Spit, the ebb tide runs from SE. to E. by S.; flood about opposite; therefore a careful attention must be paid to the current when on this line. The course from SW. Spit buoy to a little North of the Sandy Hook Point buoy is S. by E., distance 1¾ miles. The Gedney's Channel entrance buoy (P. S.) bears from SW. Spit E. ¼ S., distance 4⅞ miles; and from Sandy Hook buoy it bears E. ¼ N., distance 3⅛ miles. *Sandy Hook Light Ship* bears from the Hook buoy E.SE., distance 6⅜ miles.

The South Channel P. S. buoy is on the same bearing from the Hook buoy, distance 2¼ miles; *Sandy Hook Light Ship* bears from the Romer Beacon SE. ¾ E., distance 7¾ miles. This bearing is directly over the shoalest part of the Romer shoal.

When running in for the Swash Channel from the *Hook Light Ship*, it will not do to make your course anything North of NW. by W.

The Scotland Light Ship bears from the Hook buoy SE., distance 3 miles; and from Romer beacon SE. by S. ¼ S., distance 5⅛ miles.

Sandy Hook Light Ship bears from the Scotland E. ¼ S., distance 3⅝ miles.

There is an automatic signal buoy placed ⅛ of a mile E. by S. from Gedney's Channel entrance buoy.

BEARINGS AND DISTANCES FROM NEW YORK TO SANDY HOOK, AND FROM THENCE EAST AND SOUTH.

Staten Island Light bears from West of the Battery S. by W., distance 6 miles. Sandy Hook Point Light bears from Staten Island Light S. ¾ E., distance 7¼ miles, and the Highlands of Neversink two Lights bear S. ½ E., distance 12½ miles.

On Sandy Hook there are three fixed Lights, the first called Sandy Hook Light, which is on the SW. side of the entrance to the bay; 2d, the East beacon, or Sandy Hook Point; 3d, the West beacon, on the Bay side of the Hook, NW. from the main light. *Sandy Hook Light Ship* bears from Sandy Hook Point Light E. by S. ¾ S., distance nearly 7 miles, and from the Highland Lights she bears E.NE., distance 6¼ miles. This *Light Ship* shows two red Lights. The P. S. entrance buoy to the Gedney's Channel bears from her NW. ¼ W., distance 3⅝ miles. The entrance buoy (P. S.) to the South Channel bears from this *Light Ship* W.NW., distance 4 miles; and Romer beacon bears NW. ¾ W., distance 7¾ miles. The *Scotland Light Ship* shows two white Lights. She bears from *Sandy Hook Light Ship* E. ⅟ S., distance 3⅝ miles, and from the Sandy Hook Point Light SE. ½ E., distance 3⅝ miles.

The Scotland Light Ship bears from the Highland Lights NE. ¼ N., distance 3⅝ miles; the entrance buoy to the South Channel bears from her N. ¾ W., distance 1¼ miles. From the position of this *Light Ship* the Elm Tree Beacon, or the low Light on Staten Island, for the Swash Channel range, will be open to the right of the high, or rear Light. The directions for running in on this range is to keep the low Light a little open to the left of the high one.

BEARINGS AND DISTANCES FROM SANDY HOOK LIGHT SHIP.

Fire Island Light bears E. by N., distance 31 miles. Shinnecook Light bears E. by N., distance 66 miles. Montauk Point Light bears from Shinnecock Light E. by N. ¼ N., distance 82 miles. *Nantucket South Shoal Light Ship* bears from *Sandy Hook Light Ship* East, distance 180 miles.

FIRE ISLAND INLET.

There is an automatic whistling buoy 6 miles South of Fire Island Light. The outer or entrance buoy, P. S., bears from it N. by W., distance about 5 miles. This is a first-class nun buoy in summer, and a first-class spar in winter. From this buoy steer North to the inner bar buoy, P. S. (nun), and from thence N. by W. ¼ W. to the first spar buoy (P. S.), and from this to the second spar buoy (P. S.) steer N. by W. ½ W. The next buoy is red ; it bears from the last P. S. buoy NE. by E. You will leave this on your starboard hand, then steer E. by S. ½ S., toward the fourth spar buoy, which is black ; leave this on your port hand, and steer East along shore, and you have good anchorage. These directions are according to the latest reports.

The buoys are changed to correspond with the changes of the channel.

Sailing Directions for Little Egg Harbor, according to Location of the Buoys, January 1, 1878.—There are constant changes in the channels of all the coast inlets, but the buoys will be changed accordingly, and at all times when in their proper positions will bear the same relation to one another and the channel, *i. e.*, marking mid channel, and so placed that the run must be from one buoy to the other, until to or into the harbor.

Bring Tucker's Beach Light to bear N. by E., and run for it until to the outer buoy, a P. S. can ; from this, steer N. by W. ½ W. for the second P. S. can buoy ; then steer N. by W. for the third P. S. can buoy (between the second and third buoys there is only 7 feet of water at low tide) ; from the third, steer N. by E. for the fourth P. S. can or wooden tub, then steer N.NW. for the fifth buoy, P. S. a wooden tub; from this, the course is N. by W. for the sixth P. S. can buoy, then N. ½ E. for the seventh, a P. S. can buoy, and from the seventh steer N. by E. until abreast of the eighth buoy, which is an H. S. spar buoy on the lower end of the Middle Ground. There is good anchorage on either side of this Middle Ground, which is about 200 yards wide in the center of it.

ABSECOM INLET.

At this time, January 1, 1878, Absecom Inlet is easy of access for vessels not drawing more than 9 feet of water. Bring Absecom Light to bear W.NW., and run for it until to the outer buoy, a P. S. can, then from that, steer NW. by N. for the second P. S. buoy (can). Between the first and second buoys the depth of water at low tide is 10 feet. From the second steer NW. for the third P. S. buoy (nun), then steer N. by W. for the fourth, a P. S. nun, and from it run in for the anchorage, with no obstructions in the channel.

GREAT EGG HARBOR INLET.

The outer buoy, a P. S. can, bears from Absecom Light SW., and it lies something more than two miles from the entrance to the Inlet. From this entrance buoy steer W. NW. for the second P. S. can buoy. (Between the second and outer buoys there is 7 feet of water at low tide.) From this buoy steer NW. by W. for the third P. S. nun, then steer NW. by N. for the fourth, a P. S. nun, and from that haul to W.SW. for the fifth buoy, a P. S. spar, then steer NW. by W. for sixth buoy, a P. S. spar, then steer from that NW. by N. for the seventh, a P. S. spar, and from this buoy steer NW. for a good anchorage.

The buoys of this Inlet are about ¼ of a mile apart.

NEW JERSEY BEACH TO DELAWARE BAY.

Barnegat Light bears from *Sandy Hook Light Ship* S.SW., distance 42 miles. From Fire Island Light it bears SW., distance 65 miles, and from Shinnecock Light SW. ¾ W., distance 97 miles; from Montauk Point Light it bears SW. by W. ¼ W., distance 128 miles.   Tucker's Island, or Little Egg Harbor Light, bears from Barnegat SW. by S., distance 17½ miles.   Absecom Light bears from Barnegat SW. ¾ S., distance 28 miles.

Five Fathom Bank Light Ship bears from Barnegat SW. by S. ½ S., distance 59 miles, and from Absecom Light it bears S.SW., distance 31½ miles.   Cape May Light bears from *Five Fathom Light Ship* W. by N. ¾ N., distance 17¼ miles, and Cape Henlopen Light bears from it W. ¾ S., distance 23½ miles.

The shoal part of Five Fathom Bank bears from the *Light Ship* NW. ½ N., distance 2¼ miles.   It has a black can buoy on it.   Montauk Point Light bears from this *Light Ship* NE. ¼ E., distance 184 miles.

Hereford Light bears from the *Five Fathom Light Ship* NW. ½ N., distance 12½ miles.

COURSES TO THE DELAWARE CAPES.

From the Highland Lights bearing West, distance 2½ miles, a S. by W. ¼ W. course will take you off Barnegat, distant 3 miles, when it bears West; steer SW. by S. ¼ S., distance 24 miles, when Absecom Light will bear W. ¾ S., distance 7 miles; then steer SW. ¾ W. if bound for Delaware Bay, and you should pass Hereford Inlet Light, distance 1½ miles.

To enter the Delaware by the Cape May Channel.—When to Hereford Light keep about 1½ miles from the shore until you bring Cape May Light to bear NW. by W., then run for it until the West part of the town bears North, or to the South buoy on Old Eph Shoal, when you will gradually haul around toward the Point Buoy (red), (course about W. by N. ½ N.,) until it bears W. by N.; pass it close aboard.   (This is the shoalest part of the Channel.)

After passing the Point buoy, your course is NW. ½ N. to the Fair Way Buoy (a perpendicular striped buoy); continue on this NW. ½ N. course, and it will take you into Ship Channel, passing Mia Maul Shoal on your starboard hand. There is a large red can buoy on this shoal.

You can enter the Ship Channel, if when about five miles above the Point buoy you steer NW. by W. ½ W.; give Brandywine a good berth, and enter the channel little above the *Fourteen Foot Light Ship.*

Brandywine Light bears from Cape May NW. by W. ½ W., distance 8 miles.

Cape Henlopen Light bears from Cape May Light SW. by W., distance 10 miles.

Directions for Delaware Breakwater Harbor.—Bring Cape Henlopen Light to bear W. by S., and run in for the point of the Cape. The shore is quite bold North of the Point Light. You can enter the harbor by the South end or through between the two breakwaters, according to the wind. The best anchorage is close to the main work with the Breakwater Light bearing N. by W. The Shears buoy bears from the Breakwater Light N. by E., distance nearly 1¾ miles.

When running to or from the breakwater up the bay, keep the main Cape Henlopen Light and the Point Light in range, or East of their range, until the Breakwater Light bears SW. by S. ½ S., before hauling toward the breakwater. Those Lights in range will take you clear of the Shears, and the Brown Shoal a little East of them.

Directions to Enter Delaware Bay from the Eastward; Ship Channel.—If you are near the *Five Fathom Bank Light Ship,* steer about W. by S. and keep Cape Henlopen Light on that bearing until it is distant 3½ miles. Cape May Light will then bear N. by E. ½ E.

If you are well in to the Cape May shore—say two miles

from the land little East of the town—you can steer SW. by W., and keep Cape Henlopen Light on that bearing until within 3½ miles of it. (On this bearing you will be inside of McCrie's Shoal, which has on it a red can buoy. It will be necessary to be careful if the tide is flood, but if the Light is kept on that bearing you will go clear of all the shoals and not find less than 8¼ fathoms of water.) You, will then steer N. by W. ¾ W., distance 12 or 13 miles, to Brandywine Shoal Light. On this course you will pass to the Eastward of the Brown Shoal and West of Brandywine Light; this Light bears from the buoy on the Brown N.NE., distance 3½ miles.

The Brown bears from Cape Henlopen Main Light N. by E. ¼ E., distance 9 miles.

From Brandywine Light, *i. e.*, little West of it, the course is N.NW. ¼ W. to Cross Ledge Light, distance 12 miles. On this course you will pass East of the *Fourteen Foot Light Ship* and West of Cross Ledge Light.

January, 1878, there is an H. S. Buoy on the wreck of the schooner Addie Walton, in mid-channel, near the upper end of Joe Flogger Shoal.

The Fourteen Foot Light Ship bears from Brandywine Light NW. by W., distance 5¼ miles.

From West of Cross Ledge Light (near to it) the course to Ship John Shoal Light is NW. by N., distance 10¾ miles. This Light you will leave on your starboard hand, then steer NW. ¾ N. toward the Port Penn Range Lights, which you will bring in range and run for them until the Range Lights at Finn's Point are in line, when you will run for them in range until the Newcastle Range Lights are in line, which you will run for in range until the Deep Water Point Range Lights come in line, when you will run for them and give the shore or front Light a good berth on your starboard hand, when it will be best to work toward Wilmington Light, and keep the West side of the river best aboard until to

Tinicum Island, little above Chester ; this you will pass on your port hand.   I will end my directions here.

The Port Penn Range Lights are located to the Westward of the Reedy Island Light, which is discontinued.   These ranges take you but a little distance West of Baker's Shoal, which has a red buoy on it.

The Finn's Point Range Lights are located on New Jersey shore East of the Pea Patch, and if you wish to go toward Delaware City or West of the Pea Patch, you should keep toward the West shore little before the Newcastle Range Lights are in line, in order to clear the shoal below the Pea Patch, with an H. S. buoy on it.

The Newcastle Range Lights are on the Delaware side, 1¾ miles below Newcastle.   This range, in connection with the Deep Water Point Range Lights, marks the channel from below Pea Patch, East of the Bulkhead Shoals.   The point of intersection is on the West side of the channel, in about 18 feet of water; and vessels drawing that depth must be careful to change from one range to the other little before they come directly in line, which will keep you to the Eastward of the intersecting point, where there is ample room and a good channel.

DISTANCES AND BEARINGS FROM THE DELAWARE TO CHESAPEAKE BAY.

Fenwick Island Light bears from *Five Fathom Bank Light Ship* SW. ¼ W., distance 31 miles ; and from Cape Henlopen Light it bears S. ¼ W., distance 20 miles.   *Winter Quarter Shoal Light Ship* bears from *Five Fathom Bank Light Ship* SW. by S. ¾ S., distance 56½ miles.

From *Winter Quarter Shoal Light Ship* Chincoteague Light bears W. by S., distance 13¼ miles ; and Hog Island Light bears from it SW. ¼ W., distance 44½ miles ; Smith's Island Light bears about SW., distance 62 miles ; and Cape Henry Light bears SW. ½ S., distance 76 miles.

Shoals between Cape Henlopen and Chincoteague.—The Hen and Chickens Shoal is near Cape Henlopen (least water on it, 5 feet). There is a black spar buoy on the outer end of it, and in the channel between the North end of it and the beach there is a P. S. (or channel buoy) which you will pass close aboard on either hand ; this P. S. buoy is nearly abreast of the beacon, or Point Light, on the Cape. This shoal is about two miles long, and the South end of it is about ¼ of a mile from the shore, with a good passage West of the Shoal, by running pretty close along the beach.

Fenwick Island Shoal bears from Fenwick Island Light from E. ½ S. to E. ½ N., distance 5½ miles ; least water on it, 15 feet ; it is about 2 miles long. There is an H. S. Nun buoy near the edge of this shoal. The Isle of Wight Shoal bears from Fenwick Island Light SE. ¼ E., distance 7¼ miles. There is a second-class Can buoy (H. S.) on this shoal. It lies S. ¼ W., distance 4½ miles from Fenwick Shoal buoy. Least water on this shoal, 18 feet. Little Gull Bank Shoal bears from Fenwick Island Light S. ¾ W., distance from the Light 10½ miles, and from the shore 1½ miles. The center of Great Gull Shoal bears from Little Gull S. by E., distance 2½ miles.

Winter Quarter Shoal Can Buoy (H. S.) bears from *Winter Quarter Light Ship* NW. by W. ½ W., distance 2 miles. Least water on this Shoal, 12 feet. Black Fish Bank Shoal bears from *Winter Quarter Light Ship* SW. ¾ W., distance 9½ miles to the middle of the shoal. The West edge of this shoal bears from Chincoteague Light from S.SE. to E. ¾ S., distance 5½ miles.

Sailing Directions from the Delaware to Chesapeake Bay.— At this date, Jan. 1, 1878, there is a Green Can buoy on the wreck of the bark Cienfuegos, which, according to the bearings given in the Buoy List, is distant from Cape Henlopen Light about 2 miles ; and little outside of Hen and Chickens Shoal.

From near this buoy, or about 2 miles distance from Cape Henlopen Point, a South, little Easterly, course will take you clear of all these shoals mentioned before. You will pass West of Fenwick Island shoal and Isle of Wight Shoal, and East of the Gull Shoals on this course. You should pass Fenwick Island Light about 2 miles distance ; and if so, continue the same course until *Winter Quarter Shoal Light Ship* bears SW. by W. ; you can then run for, and pass, the *Light Ship* as you choose ; and from her, a S. ¾ W. course will take you to the Chesapeake, passing Hog Island Light at a distance of 5 miles, and Smith's Island about 3½ miles distance.

If you would feel safe in regard to the shoals North of Chincoteague, you must observe carefully the bearings and distances given ; or do not get into less than 14 fathoms of water.

Sailing Directions for Chesapeake Bay Ship Channel.— Bring Cape Henry Light to bear SW. by W., and run for it until it is distant 3½ miles, when Smith Island Light will bear N. by E.; you will then steer NW. ½ W. about 12 miles, when Thimble Shoal Light will bear SW. by W., distance 5½ miles, and Back River Light will bear W. by N. ¼ N., distance 5¼ miles. The course from this to Smith's Point Light is North, distance 49 miles.

To enter Chesapeake Bay by the North Channel.—Bring Smith's Island Light to bear North, distance from 2½ to 3 miles, and steer W. ¼ S. (or make that course), keeping the breakers on your starboard hand about ¾ to 1 mile distant, and you will pass about midway of the Isaacs and Nautilus Shoal. You can continue on this W. ¼ S. course, and pass over the Middle Ground in 16 to 18 feet of water ; or when 3 miles West of the Isaacs, you can steer NW. by W., and go between the Middle Ground Shoals ; or when three-fourths of a mile past the Isaacs, you can steer N. by W. ¼ W., passing about three-eighths of a mile West of Fisherman's Island ; when you have run about 5 miles on this course, steer NW. and proceed up the Bay. This last direction will take you East of the Inner Middle Ground, and it is not very safe for a stranger.

DIRECTIONS FOR HAMPTON ROADS AND NORFOLK.

When Cape Henry Light bears SW. by W., distance 2½ miles, steer W. by N. ¼ N. for the Thimble Shoal Light, which is a hexagonal screw-pile Lighthouse in 11 feet water at low tide, located on the shoalest point of the Thimble, and distant 3½ miles from Old Point Comfort Light. The iron foundation of the Lighthouse is painted brown, and the superstructure drab. To the Southward of the Light the water deepens rapidly to 8 and 9 fathoms; there is a 10 foot lump about 700 yards to the Westward. The Lighthouse to be left on the starboard hand going into Hampton Roads.

The Thimble Shoal Light is 16¾ miles from Cape Henry; bearing from it NW. by W. ½ W. when opposite this Light or when it bears North, the course is W. by S. ¾ S. into the Roads.

If bound to Norfolk, after passing Fort Monroe docks, steer SW. by S. ½ S., distance 4 miles, to a red can buoy, which you pass on the starboard hand; the course from this to Crancy Island Light is South 4¾ miles, then steer toward Lambert Point Light, which you pass on the port hand; steer then about for the Light on Naval Hospital wharf, keeping near to Fort Norfolk. Good anchorage about West of the Naval Hospital dock.

Lambert Point Light is a square screw-pile Lighthouse in 6 feet of water on the shoal making off from Lambert's Point. The iron foundation is red, the superstructure white. Boats drawing more than 5 feet of water should not pass to Eastward of the Lighthouse. There is a pile of stone ballast 50 yards in a Southerly direction from the Light, which is nearly bare at low water.

CHESAPEAKE BAY AND BALTIMORE.

When bound up the Chesapeake Bay, from six miles E.SE. of Back River Light, the course to Smith's Point Light is North, and the following Lights will be passed in the order given. York Spit Light bears from Back River N. ¾ E., dis-

tance 7¼ miles; Toos Marsh Light on the East side of the
Bay, bears from York Spit E. by N. ½ N., distance 11 miles.
New Point Comfort Light bears from York Spit N. by W.,
distance 6 miles; the Wolf Trap Light bears from York
Spit N. by E. ½ E., distance 11 miles.

Stingray Point Light bears from Wolf Trap N. by W. ¾ W.,
distance 11 miles.

Windmill Point Light bears from Wolf Trap N. by W.,
distance 13¼ miles.

Smith's Point Light bears from Windmill Point Light N.
¾ E., distance 18 miles.

The next course from Smith's Point Light is N. by W. ½
W. for 51 miles, when Sharp's Island Light on the East side
will bear SE. ½ E., distant a little over 6 miles. On this
course you will pass Point Lookout Light, which bears from
Smith's Point NW. by N. ¼ N., distance 10¼ miles.

Cove Point Light bears from Smith's Point N. by W. ½ W.,
distance 31 miles.

From the above bearing of Sharp's Island Light, the course
is N. by E. ½ E., until up to Sandy Point Light, distance 20
miles. (Before you get to this Light, you pass Thomas Point
Shoal Light, which is 7½ miles below Sandy Point.) When
up to Sandy Point, pass it distant one mile on port hand, then
steer about North, for the Craighill channel Range Lights.
These two Lights are designed as Leading or Range Lights
for the Craighill channel; the one near Miller's Island is
distant from North Point in a Northeasterly direction, about
3¾ nautical miles; the other 2¼ nautical miles, East by South
from North Point. These two Lights are 2½ nautical miles
apart, bearing due North and South from each other, and
they are exactly in range with the axis of the Craighill channel. The front (or low) Lighthouse is in 15 feet of water
at mean low tide, and will show above the water as a cast-
iron cylinder, surmounted by the keeper's dwelling and

lantern. The focal plane is 30 feet above the level of the Bay at mean low water. The rear (or high) Lighthouse is an open frame pyramid of four sides, the lower portion being painted straw color, and the upper part black. The lens of the rear (or high) Light is a range lens, and will be seen only in the direction of the axis of the Craighill channel. They should both be distinctly visible below the South end of the channel in ordinary states of the atmosphere. When a vessel is on the true course going up or down stream, the two Lights will show one directly over the other, a slight change to either side producing a corresponding change in the relative position of the Lights. Keep up on this range until the Hawkins' Point and Leading Point Lights are in range.

The Hawkins' Point Light is a hexagonal screw-pile structure in 6 feet water, superstructure white, two Lights, one above the other. This Lighthouse, and the one on Leading Point, are 1½ miles apart on a line bearing W.NW. ¼ W., and E.SE. ¼ E. from each other, both designed to serve as a range for the Brewerton channel. When a vessel is on the true course coming up or going down the Brewerton channel, the three (3) Lights—two (2) on structure near Hawkins' Point, and one (1) on structure on Leading Point—will be seen in line one above the other; but whenever this course is departed from, however slightly, to port or starboard, a corresponding change in the position of the Lights will be observed. Steer for these Lights until the Light on Fort Carroll bears NW. by N., then haul up to that course, passing Fort Carroll on the starboard hand. When about one mile above the Fort, keep the Lazaretto Point Light open on the starboard bow, and pass it on the starboard hand, leaving Fort McHenry on the port. After passing this Fort, you will pass a black buoy on the port hand, then steer about NW. by N. and anchor above the coal docks.

A DESCRIPTION OF SOME OF THE LIGHTHOUSES IN THE CHESAPEAKE BAY.

York Spit is a screw-pile Lighthouse, placed in 12½ feet water at mean low tide; iron piles painted red, and the superstructure yellow.   Serves as a guide up and down the Bay. Vessels drawing over 24 feet of water should not approach this Lighthouse on the Eastern side nearer than one-half mile. Vessels drawing not over 18 feet water may approach the Light on the East side within a quarter of a mile, and on the South and Southwest within three-quarters of a mile, and vessels drawing not over 14 feet may pass over the shoal to the Northwestward of the Light within one-quarter of a mile. New Point Comfort Light (fixed white) bears N. by W., distance 5½ nautical miles, and Back River Light (revolving white) bears S. by W., distance 7¼ nautical miles.

The Wolf Trap is a screw-pile Lighthouse, placed in 12½ feet water at mean low tide.   The iron piles of the foundation are painted *red*, and the superstructure *lead color*.   Stingaray Point Light (red) bears N. by W. ¾ W., distant 10¾ miles. New Point Comfort Light (white) bears SW. ½ S., distant 6¾ miles; guide up the Bay.

Windmill Point Light is a screw-pile Lighthouse, in 12 feet water at mean tide.   Stingaray Point Light (fixed red) bears SW. by S., distant about 2 miles.   Vessels drawing 18 feet or more should not approach the Lighthouse on Eastern side nearer than 2 nautical miles; vessels drawing less than 18 feet may approach the Light on the North or South side within 1,000 yards with safety; and vessels drawing 12 feet or less may approach it in safety to within 400 yards on the North, East, and South sides, but should not attempt to pass between it and the land at Windmill Point.   A first-class buoy (No. 9), painted black, and properly numbered, marks the Eastern extremity of the Spit making out from Windmill Point.

Smith's Point Light is a screw-pile structure in 12 feet of water at mean low tide, with from 4 to 6 fathoms on the shoal extending about one mile all around from NW. to SW. by the W'd.   Vessels drawing from 12 to 14 feet of water may approach the Lighthouse safely within a distance of 250 yards, but vessels of a heavier draught should give it a berth of one-third of a mile.

7

Point Lookout Light is on the North side of the entrance to Potomac River.

Light on keeper's dwelling-house painted white; roof of lantern red.

Thomas Point Light is a screw-pile structure, white; lantern red; stands in 8 feet of water.

Sandy Point Light, on keeper's red-brick dwelling; shoals make out nearly a mile from this Light, and vessels drawing more than 10 feet of water should not approach nearer than that.

Love Point Light bears E.NE. from Sandy Point Light, distance 5 miles; it is on the East side of the bay, and serves as a guide to Chester River. Vessels drawing more than 9 feet of water should not pass between the Light and the Point.

Seven-Foot Knoll Light is an octagonal screw-pile structure, between the Main and Swash channels; it bears from Sandy Point North, distance 8½ miles; and from Love Point NW. ½ N., distance 8 miles; and from the South Light of the Craighill channel about S. by W. ½ W.

Sailing Directions for the Potomac River.—From one mile North of Smith's Point Light steer NW. ½ W., distance about 21 miles, up to Piney Point Light, passing it on your starboard hand, and when it bears NE., distance one mile, steer NW. ¼ N. about 4 miles, to clear Ragged Point, off which there is a black buoy; pass it on your port hand, and when it bears South steer W. by N. ¼ N. for 10½ miles, passing Blackston Island Light about ⅝ of a mile distant on your starboard hand.

This course should take you up to the first channel, or P. S. buoy on the Kettle Bottoms; pass this buoy close aboard on your starboard hand, then steer NW. by W. ¼ W., distance 3¼ miles, passing two buoys on your starboard hand, and when past the second one, steer NW. ¼ W., distance 3⅝ miles, passing two buoys on your starboard, and the third one on your port; this is the last of the Kettle Bottom buoys, and if in their places, you will find the best water by passing them in the order here given. When little above the last buoy named, steer NW. by W., distance 2½ miles, passing a can buoy close aboard; from this buoy to Lower Cedar Point Light the course is N. by W. ½ W., distance 3½ miles; before you get to the Light you will pass a red buoy on Cedar Point Shoal; pass this on your starboard hand, and the Lighthouse on your port. When to this Light, steer N. ½ W., until Mathias Point Light bears NW. by W. ½ W., when you will run for it open on your port, passing it on that hand, and when past it about ¼ of a mile, keep the Fog Signal Station off Cedar Point open on your starboard bow, passing it on that hand; course about W. by S. ½ S., up toward the Maryland shore; then follow up the red buoys until around Maryland Point. After getting well around the Point, or to Lower Thomas Point, the best water is nearer to the Maryland shore up to Sandy Point; from off this Point steer N. by E. about 3 miles, or until ¼ of a mile above the red buoy off Chicomuxen Creek, when you will steer NE. for Indian Head, distance nearly 6 miles; you will pass a P. S. and a black buoy on this run. The shore is quite bold at Indian Head, and you will keep that shore until Craney Island, a fishing place, bears NW., when you can steer N. ½ E., passing close by Hallowing Point on your port hand; this course will take you to White Stone Point, when you will gradually work off to E.NE., passing the White House (a summer resort) about ¼ of a mile before you get on this course, which will take you to Fort Washington on the Maryland shore, distance from the White House 4⅞ miles. From Fort Washington to Jones' Point Light the course first is N. ½ E., distance 2¾ miles; then North 1⅞ miles, to the Light. On this run of 4½ miles the channel is quite narrow, and the flats extend well off from the West shore, but if the buoys are watched, a stranger can find his way up to Alexandria by these directions, if he has any kind of a chart that will show the make of the river.

I have not thought it necessary to give all the buoys in detail as passed, with these general directions, as the colors of the buoys are expected to speak for themselves.

Distances and Bearings from Cape Henry to Cape Fear, N. C. —Currituck Beach Light bears from Cape Henry Light S. by E., distance 34 miles.

Body's Island Light bears from Currituck Beach Light S. by E. ¾ E., distance 34½ miles, and from Cape Henry Light it bears S. by E. ¼ E., distance 70 miles.

Cape Hatteras Light bears from Body's Island South, distance 35 miles.

Ocracoke Light bears SW. by W. ½ W. from Hatteras Light, distance 23½ miles.

Cape Lookout Light bears from Cape Hatteras about SW. ½ W., distance 63 miles.

Frying Pan Shoal Light Ship bears from Cape Lookout SW. ¼ W., distance 87 miles.

The distance from Cape Hatteras to Montauk Point (straight line) is 400 miles.

These bearings given have no reference to Sailing Directions.

NOTES.

When vessels are close hauled, the one on the port tack is expected to give way to those on the starboard tack, unless by so doing she will risk collision with another vessel, or run ashore by giving way. The side which the wind blows on, either starboard or port, is the tack that the vessel is on. This rule is too simple to be forgotten.

I hope the steamers will adopt the custom of sounding the whistle to pass sailing vessels, when there can be a doubt in the mind of the vessel's captain which side the steamer desires to take, both day and night.

TABLE

Showing the Amount of One Day's Wages, from One Dollar per Month to One Hundred, allowing Thirty Days for a Month, as the General Custom is with Seamen.

Where the exact amount is not given, add the number wanted to get the desired sum, that is, from one to five dollars per month.

Wages per Month.	One Day.	Wages per Month.	One Day.
$1.00	$.03⅓	$45.00	$1.50
2.00	.06⅔	50.00	1.66⅔
3.00	.10	55.00	1.83⅓
4.00	.13⅓	60.00	2.00
5.00	.16⅔	65.00	2.16⅔
10.00	.33⅓	70.00	2.33⅓
15.00	.50	75.00	2.50
20.00	.66⅔	80.00	2.66⅔
25.00	.83⅓	85.00	2.83⅓
30.00	1.00	90.00	3.00
35.00	1.16⅔	95.00	3.16⅔
40.00	1.33⅓	100.00	3.33⅓

PICKLE FOR SAILS.

The best preparation to prevent mildew in sails and awnings that I have yet found, is mixed, and used as follows: For a schooner's sails of 150 tons O. M., take about one peck of good lime, slack it with a little water, then add from 10 to 20 pounds of pulverized alum, and not less than 4 bushels of salt. Mix in a hogshead if you can, fill it with fresh water, and keep the mixture well stirred when using it. Scrub both sides of the sails, then roll them up as snug as possible, and let them remain rolled and covered not less than 24 hours, but one week if possible, keeping the sun from them. I recommend fresh water, as I think it is the best.

To do this work on a sand beach is a very hard task for all hands, and for the benefit of some, I will recommend Essex on the Connecticut river, as the best and most convenient place for this work that there is on the coast, as there is a dock, part of which is used for that purpose, always clean, and no lifting and boating sails required.

For smaller sails, keep nearly the quantity of alum, and plenty of salt—in fact, use all that the water will dissolve. Alum that is not pulverized dissolves very slowly.

TO YACHTMEN, COASTERS, AND SHIP CAPTAINS.

At Seeley & Stevens', No. 32 Burling Slip, you will find the best Spar and Bright Work Composition that can be found for inside or outside use.

At C. H. Pratt's, No. 34 Burling Slip, can be found the best quality of Hemp and Manila Rope at *coil* prices, for any length. Also a full assortment of Ship and Yacht Stores.

At Fiske & Westen's, No. 36 Burling Slip, you will find Capt. Pepper's Signal Oil ; the best in the market.

At T. S. & J. D. Negus', No. 140 Water street, a full supply of Nautical Instruments, Books, Charts, &c., can be found ; also, the Yachtman and Coaster's Book of Reference.

MEMORANDA.

Office of the Chief Signal Officer,

WASHINGTON, D. C., January 1, 1878.

CIRCULAR.

On and after January 1, 1878, an additional Cautionary Storm Signal will be displayed, as occasion may require, at all active Signal and Display stations of the Signal Service. The signal will be displayed at and on the regular place and staff, and will consist of *a white flag with a square black centre*, shown above *a red flag with a square black centre* by day, or a *white light* shown above a *red light* by night. This signal will be known as the "CAUTIONARY OFF-SHORE SIGNAL," and will indicate, when shown, that while the storm disturbance is considered, at the office of the Chief Signal Officer, as not yet passed for the port or place at which the signal is displayed, and the winds may yet be high, and there may be danger, the winds are expected to blow from a northern or western direction, or "off-shore," at or near the port or place where the signal may be.

The display of this signal will often follow, and must be distinguished from, the display of the usual "Cautionary Signal," *i. e.*, a square red flag with a square black centre by day, or a red light shown at night—which retains, whenever shown alone, its usual meaning. The display of either signal is always cautionary.

The "CAUTIONARY SIGNAL," *i. e.*, a red flag with black square in the centre by day, or a red light by night, calls for caution in view of an approaching storm, and is so "CAUTIONARY" WITH REFERENCE TO WINDS BLOWING FROM ANY DIRECTION.

The CAUTIONARY OFF-SHORE SIGNAL, *i. e.*, a white flag with black square in the centre, shown above a red flag with black square in the centre, by day, or a white light shown above a red light by night, is "CAUTIONARY" WITH REFERENCE TO WINDS EXPECTED TO BLOW FROM A NORTHERN OR WESTERN DIRECTION, OR OFF-SHORE AT OR NEAR THE PLACE AT WHICH IT MAY BE.

Albert J. Myer

Brig. Gen. (Bvt. Assg'd,) Chief Signal Officer, U. S. A.

POST THIS UP IN A CONSPICUOUS PLACE.

MEMORANDA.

THE CAUTIONARY SIGNAL.
Cautionary against Approaching Storm, and against Winds
from any direction.

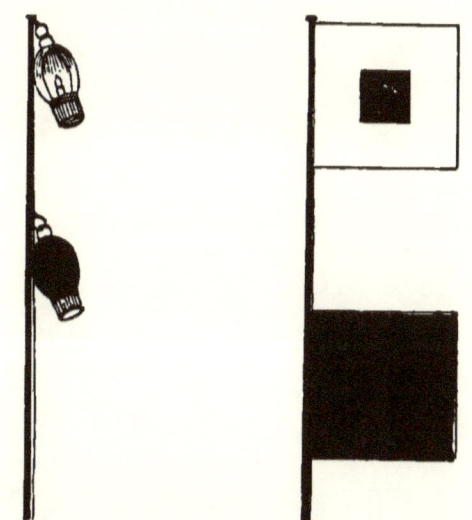

THE CAUTIONARY OFF-SHORE SIGNAL.
Cautionary against Rough Weather, and against Winds expected
to be in a Northern or Western direction, or "Off-Shore."

The order "Up Signals" retains its present meaning.

The order "Hoist Off-shore Signal" requires that the "Off-shore Signal" be at once displayed, the "Cautionary Signal" being either lowered, and the two flags or two lights of the "Off-shore Signal" hoisted in its place, or the flag or light of the "Cautionary Signal" may be left displayed, while the additional proper flag or light needed to complete the "Off-shore Signal" is shown above it.

"Signals Down" lowers any or all signals.